AF480311

OCTOBER EVER AFTER PUBLISHING
WHERE EVERY STORY FINDS A HEART

TIMELESS CONNECTIONS

∞

Timeless Connections

A Novel by

Robert Anthony Newsome-White

Dedication

To my beloved husband, Thomas, for your unwavering encouragement, endless inspiration, and the love that gives my words meaning.

This journey would not be possible without you by my side.

With all my heart,

Robert

Table of Contents

Chapter 1: Reunion Sparks

The room buzzed with the low hum of chatter and the occasional burst of laughter. Ryan hesitated just inside the entrance of the high school gymnasium, his fingers tightening around the strap of his leather messenger bag. The familiar scent of polished wood floors mingled with the faint aroma of punch and hors d'oeuvres. Memories stirred—locker room banter, the thrill of football games, and peaceful afternoons spent in the library.

Ryan had always been the shy one, the kid who blended into the background, but tonight was different. Tonight, he wasn't just a teenager trying to figure out who he was. He was a man who had fought to claim his identity, scars and all. Yet, as he scanned the room, searching for familiar faces among the clusters of alumni, a tight knot of nerves formed in his stomach.

And then, he saw him.

David stood near a table stacked with yearbooks, engaged in a lively conversation with a group of former classmates. His laugh, warm and unmistakable, cut through the ambient noise, sending a ripple of emotion through Ryan. Time had etched a few lines on David's face, but it had also added a confident ease to his posture. His hair, once boyishly tousled, was now neatly styled, and the way he carried himself spoke of someone comfortable in his own skin.

Ryan froze, his heart racing as if he were seventeen again. In those days, David had been the star athlete, effortlessly charming and magnetic. They had shared countless moments that bordered on something deeper—stolen glances, lingering touches during a game of basketball, conversations that stretched late into the night. But they had never dared to cross the unspoken line.

Now, years later, their eyes met across the crowded room. For a moment, the noise and the people faded away. Ryan saw recognition flicker in David's expression, followed by something else—something Ryan couldn't quite name but felt deep in his chest. Slowly, David excused himself from the group and began walking toward him.

Ryan's pulse quickened with every step David took. What would he say? What could he say after all these years? A thousand rehearsed greetings dissolved into incoherence as David finally stopped in front of him.

"Ryan," David said, his voice warm and laced with nostalgia. "It's been too long."

"David." Ryan managed a smile, his voice steadier than he felt. "Yeah, it has."

David's eyes, a shade of hazel Ryan had memorized long ago, softened as they shook hands. "I almost didn't recognize you. You look… good."

Ryan chuckled nervously, his fingers brushing the edges of his bag. "You too. It's good to see you."

The exchange felt both casual and monumental, as if they were balancing on the edge of something profound. They lapsed into a momentary silence, the weight of their shared history filling the space between them.

Around them, classmates mingled, music played, and the reunion unfolded, but neither seemed inclined to rejoin the crowd.

"Want to get some air?" David asked, motioning toward the exit.

Ryan nodded, grateful for the suggestion. They slipped out into the crisp night, the cool breeze a welcome contrast to the stuffy gymnasium. The school parking lot stretched before them, bathed in the glow of streetlights. They found a bench near the edge of the property, where the hum of the reunion was little more than a muffled backdrop.

"So," David began, leaning forward with his elbows on his knees, "what have you been up to all these years?"

Ryan hesitated, debating how much to share. "A lot, I guess. Moved around a bit, worked different jobs, tried to figure out who I am."
David nodded thoughtfully. "I get that. Life doesn't

exactly come with a manual, does it?"

Ryan smiled faintly. "No, it doesn't."

They talked, cautiously at first, but with increasing ease
as the minutes turned into hours. Ryan shared snippets of
his life, leaving out the parts that still felt too raw. David,
in turn, spoke of his career, his travels, and the
challenges he had faced. Somewhere in the exchange,
the years that had separated them began to dissolve,
replaced by a familiar rhythm that felt like coming home.

As the night deepened, their conversation grew easier,
more introspective. David's gaze lingered on Ryan his
expression unreadable. "You know," he said softly, "I've
thought about you over the years. Wondered where you
were, how you were doing."

Ryan's breath hitched. "You have?"

David nodded, a small smile playing at the corners of his
lips. "Yeah. You were… essential to me back then."

Ryan's chest tightened. The vulnerability in David's voice was like a key turning in a lock he hadn't realized was still closed. For years, he had buried his feelings for David, convincing himself they were one-sided. But now, sitting here under the stars, he couldn't ignore the possibility that David had felt the same.

"I've thought about you too," Ryan admitted, his voice barely above a whisper. "More than I should have."

David's smile widened, and for a moment, they simply sat there, the unspoken words between them heavy with possibility.

That night, as they said their goodbyes and exchanged phone numbers, Ryan felt a spark of hope he hadn't felt in years. The reunion, once a source of anxiety, had become a turning point. For the first time in a long time, he allowed himself to believe that something extraordinary might be waiting just around the corner.

Chapter 2: Igniting the Past

The following days after the reunion passed in a haze for Ryan. The weight of reconnecting with David pressed against his thoughts, softening the edges of his routine. He'd replayed their conversations in his mind, savoring the moments of connection and wondering what their renewed relationship might mean. The phone number David had given him sat on his nightstand, a beacon of possibility.

After a few days of internal debate, Ryan finally worked up the courage to send a text. The message was simple:

"Hey, it's Ryan. Great seeing you at the reunion. Hope you're doing well."

He hit send before he could second-guess himself and waited anxiously for a response. The reply came within minutes

"Hey, Ryan! I was just thinking about you. Want to grab coffee sometime this week?"

Ryan's heart leapt. The casual invitation felt like a lifeline, an opportunity to explore what had sparked between them at the reunion. He quickly typed back, agreeing to meet the following Saturday.

The coffee shop they chose was small and tucked away in a peaceful corner of town. When Ryan arrived, David was already there, seated at a corner table with a cup of steaming coffee in front of him. He looked up as Ryan approached, his face breaking into a warm smile.

"Hey," David greeted, standing to hug him. The embrace was brief but grounding, the kind that seemed to say, I'm glad you're here.

"Hey," Ryan replied, settling into the chair opposite him. The aroma of roasted coffee beans and the gentle hum of conversation surrounded them, creating a cozy cocoon.

Their conversation started easily, flowing naturally from

topic to topic. They reminisced about high school, filling in the blanks of the years they'd spent apart. David talked about his job in marketing, the cities he'd lived in, and the hobbies he'd picked up along the way. Ryan, in turn, shared stories of his time working odd jobs, his move back to their hometown, and his efforts to rebuild his life.

But beneath the surface of their casual chatter, there was a tension neither of them could ignore. It was in the way their eyes lingered a little too long, the way their hands occasionally brushed when they reached for their drinks, and the way their laughter felt like a shared secret.

When the conversation lulled, David leaned back in his chair, studying Ryan with a thoughtful expression. "You seem different from how I remember you," he said, his voice soft. "More confident, maybe. More… yourself."

Ryan felt a blush creeping up his neck. "I've changed a lot since high school. Back then, I was too afraid to really be myself."

David nodded, a hint of understanding in his gaze. "Me too. I think we all were, in some ways."

The vulnerability in his words hung between them, drawing them closer. Ryan felt a surge of courage and decided to take a chance. "Can I ask you something?"

"Of course."

"Did you ever feel like… like there was something between us back then? Something more than just friendship?"

David's eyes widened slightly, and for a moment, Ryan feared he had overstepped. But then David smiled, a slow, almost wistful smile. "Yeah," he admitted. "I did. But I didn't know what to do with it. I was scared— scared of what it meant, scared of how people would react. So, I buried it."

Ryan exhaled, relief washing over him. "I felt the same. I just didn't know if you ever noticed."

"I noticed," David said, his voice tinged with warmth. "I just wasn't ready to face it back then."

They sat in silence for a moment, the weight of their confessions settling over them. Then David reached across the table, his fingers brushing against Ryan's. It was a small gesture, but it spoke volumes.
"I'm ready now," David said, his voice steady. "If you are."

Ryan's chest tightened with a mix of fear and exhilaration. He had spent so long running from his feelings, convincing himself that they were unessential, that they didn't matter. But now, sitting across from David, he realized he didn't want to run anymore.

"I'm ready," he said, his voice barely above a whisper.

In the weeks that followed, Ryan and David's connection deepened. They met for dinners, went on long walks through the park, and spent hours talking about everything from their childhood dreams to their fears about the future. The more time they spent together, the more they realized how much they had missed each other—and how much they had to learn about the people they had become.

Late one evening, after a movie night at David's apartment, they found themselves sitting on the couch, the credits rolling on the screen. The room was quiet except for the sound of their breathing, and the tension that had been simmering between them all night finally came to a head.

"Ryan," David said, turning to face him. His eyes were earnest, his expression open. "I need to tell you something."

Ryan's heart raced. "What is it?"
David hesitated, then reached out to take Ryan's hand. "I've spent a long time trying to figure out who I am, and I'm still figuring it out. But I know one thing for sure—I want to figure it out with you."

The sincerity in his words brought tears to Ryan's eyes. For years, he had dreamed of a moment like this, but he had never dared to hope it could actually happen.

"I want that too," he said, his voice thick with emotion.

David smiled, and in that moment, all the years of fear and doubt melted away. They leaned in, their foreheads touching, and for the first time in their lives, they allowed themselves to truly be seen.

That night marked the beginning of a new chapter in their relationship. It wasn't without its challenges—old fears and insecurities lingered, and they knew they would have to navigate them together. But for the first time, they felt like they had the strength to face whatever came their way, as long as they had each other.

Chapter 3: The Awakening

Ryan awoke the next morning feeling lighter, as though a heavy weight he hadn't realized he'd been carrying had finally been lifted. The memory of David's words the night before played on a loop in his mind: "I want to figure it out with you." The sincerity in David's voice had etched itself into Ryan's heart, and for the first time in years, he felt truly seen, truly wanted.

David, too, was navigating uncharted territory. He sat at his kitchen table that morning, sipping coffee and staring out the window. He couldn't help but reflect on how far he had come. For years, he had buried the truth about himself, hiding behind a façade of casual relationships and professional accomplishments. But last night, with Ryan, he had finally started to peel back the layers. And it felt… right.

Their evolving relationship brought a new level of vulnerability for both of them. For Ryan, it meant confronting parts of himself he had kept hidden, even from his closest friends. For David, it meant unlearning years of ingrained fears about how the world might perceive him.

Their first few weeks as a couple were a mix of exhilaration and trepidation. They spent hours talking, diving into conversations that were as lighthearted as they were profound. They discussed their favorite movies, their most embarrassing high school moments, and the ways they had changed over the years. But they also ventured into deeper territory, sharing the fears and insecurities that had shaped them.

"I always felt like I didn't belong," Ryan confessed one evening as they walked along the riverfront. The golden glow of the sunset reflected on the water, casting an ethereal light on their surroundings. "Even in high school, I was constantly trying to fit into a mold that didn't feel like me."

David nodded, his hand brushing against Ryan's as they

walked. "I know what you mean. I spent so much time pretending to be someone I wasn't. It's exhausting, isn't it?"

Ryan smiled faintly. "It is. But with you… I don't feel like I have to pretend."

David stopped walking and turned to face him. The vulnerability in Ryan's voice struck a chord deep within him. Without a word, he reached out and took Ryan's hand, intertwining their fingers. It was a small gesture, but in that moment, it felt monumental.

"You don't ever have to pretend with me," David said softly. "Not now. Not ever."

As their relationship deepened, so did their understanding of themselves. For Ryan, the realization that he was gay was both liberating and daunting. He had spent so much of his life suppressing his true feelings that embracing them felt like stepping into the light after years of living in the shadows.

One night, as they sat on Ryan's couch sharing a bottle of wine, Ryan opened up about his journey of self-discovery. "I think I've always known, deep down," he admitted, staring into his glass. "But I was scared. Scared of what it would mean for my relationships, my family, my future. So, I pushed it down and tried to ignore it."

David listened intently, his gaze never leaving Ryan's face. "I get that," he said. "For a long time, I told myself it was just a phase. That if I ignored it long enough, it would go away. But it never did."

Ryan looked up, meeting David's eyes. "When did you finally accept it?"

David hesitated, thinking back to the moment his perspective shifted. "It wasn't one specific moment," he said. "It was a series of small realizations. Little things that added up over time. But meeting you again… it's like everything clicked into place. Like I finally had permission to just be myself."

Ryan smiled, his heart swelling with emotion. "You're braver than you give yourself credit for, you know."

David chuckled, shaking his head. "I don't know about that. But I do know that I'm tired of running. Tired of hiding. I just want to live my truth."

Their conversation that night marked a turning point. Together, they began exploring the intricacies of their identities, supporting each other through the highs and lows of self-discovery. They read books, watched documentaries, and attended LGBTQ+ support groups, eager to connect with others who had walked similar paths.

But their journey wasn't without its challenges. The conservative small town they had grown up in cast a long shadow, and the fear of judgment lingered in the back of their minds. At first, they kept their relationship private, sharing their truth only with a small circle of trusted friends.

One of those friends was Emily, a mutual classmate who had always been a beacon of support for both of them. When Ryan and David came out to her over coffee one afternoon, her reaction was immediate and heartfelt.

"I'm so happy for you both," she said, pulling them into a group hug. "You deserve all the love and happiness in the world."

Her unwavering support gave them the courage to take the next step: coming out to their families. The process was nerve-wracking, filled with moments of doubt and anxiety. But to their relief, most of their loved ones responded with kindness and understanding.

"It's about time," Ryan's younger cousin teased when he shared the news. "We've been rooting for you two since high school!"

Their newfound openness was liberating, but it also came with its own set of challenges. Not everyone in their lives was accepting, and the sting of rejection from certain acquaintances was a painful reminder of the prejudice they still faced.

Through it all, Ryan and David leaned on each other, their bond growing stronger with every obstacle they overcame. They discovered that the key to navigating this new chapter of their lives was honesty—both with themselves and with each other.

"I'm proud of us," Ryan said one night as they lay in bed, their hands intertwined. "For not letting fear win. For choosing each other."

David smiled, pressing a kiss to Ryan's forehead. "Me too. And I promise, no matter what happens, I'll always choose you."

Their awakening wasn't just about embracing their sexuality—it was about embracing life, love, and the endless possibilities that came with living authentically. Together, they were writing a new story, one that was unapologetically their own.

Chapter 4: Hidden Desires

As Ryan and David's relationship deepened, they found themselves treading a delicate balance between friendship and something far more profound. Every touch, every glance, and every word carried a weight they were both acutely aware of but hesitant to fully embrace. It wasn't just love—it was uncharted territory, an intoxicating blend of passion and vulnerability that neither had experienced before.

On warm summer evenings, they often found themselves at the edge of the park overlooking the small town they both called home. The air would hum with the chirping of crickets and the rustling of leaves, a symphony that seemed to echo the emotions simmering between them. Sitting side by side on a weathered bench, they would talk for hours, their conversations dipping into memories, dreams, and the fears they were learning to confront together.

"I never thought I'd feel this way," David admitted one evening, his voice barely louder than the breeze. His fingers toyed with the hem of his shirt as if searching for an anchor. "Not about anyone. And definitely not about you."

Ryan turned to him, his expression open and unguarded. "Why me?"

David hesitated, his gaze fixed on the dark horizon. "Because you see me," he said at last. "The real me. And that's terrifying."

Ryan smiled, his heart aching at the vulnerability in David's voice. "You don't have to be scared with me. I'm right here."

Despite the comfort they found in each other, the backdrop of their conservative small town loomed large, a constant reminder of the societal expectations they were defying. Whispers followed them when they walked too close together, and the weight of judgment hung heavy in the air. Ryan, who had spent most of his life blending into the background, struggled with the attention their relationship garnered. David, who had always been the charismatic center of their social circle, found himself withdrawing, unsure of how to reconcile the image others had of him with the truth of who he was.

Their late-night conversations began to take on a more serious tone as they navigated their fears and insecurities.

"What if people never accept us?" Ryan asked one night, his voice tinged with worry. They were lying on a blanket in the middle of a field, the stars above them offering a sense of solace.

David sighed, reaching out to take Ryan's hand. "They don't have to. We're not living for them. We're living for us."

The conviction in David's voice gave Ryan a measure of strength, but the doubt lingered. Could they really build a life together in a place that seemed determined to pull them apart?

Their relationship also brought to the surface desires that both had buried for years. For David, it was the realization that he had spent much of his life seeking approval from others, often at the expense of his happiness. For Ryan, it was the understanding that love could be as liberating as it was terrifying.

One night, as they prepared dinner in David's small apartment, their conversation turned to the future. "Do you ever think about leaving?" Ryan asked, his hands busy chopping vegetables. "This town, I mean."

David paused, the knife in his hand hovering over a cutting board. "All the time," he admitted. "But it's not just about leaving. It's about finding a place where we can be ourselves—where we don't have to hide."
Ryan looked up, meeting David's gaze. "Do you think that place exists?"

David smiled faintly, his eyes softening. "I think we'll

find it. Together."

Their journey wasn't without its challenges. The more they explored their feelings, the more they realized how deeply ingrained their fears were. Small moments—like holding hands in public or introducing each other to friends—felt monumental, fraught with both exhilaration and anxiety.

At one point, a confrontation with an old acquaintance forced them to confront the prejudice they had been trying to ignore. It happened on a calm afternoon at the local diner, where they had decided to grab lunch. As they sat at their booth, laughing over shared memories, a man from their high school days approached them.

"Well, isn't this something," the man said, his tone dripping with condescension. "You two… together?"

David tensed, his jaw tightening. "What's your point?"

The man shrugged, smirking. "No point. Just didn't peg

you for… this."

Ryan felt the heat rising in his cheeks, but before he could respond, David leaned forward, his voice calm but firm. "You don't have to understand it. But you will respect it."

The man faltered, caught off guard by David's confidence, before muttering something under his breath and walking away. The encounter left both Ryan and David shaken but also more determined than ever to stand up for their love.

Amidst the challenges, there were moments of pure joy that reminded them why they were fighting so hard. Like the night they danced in David's living room, the soft glow of fairy lights casting a warm hue over the space. The music was low, and the world outside felt far away as they swayed together, their laughter mingling with the melody.

Or the time they spent an entire Saturday exploring the woods behind Ryan's childhood home, their laughter echoing through the trees as they stumbled upon hidden clearings and forgotten trails. In those moments, the weight of the world lifted, leaving only the simplicity of their connection.

By the end of the summer, Ryan and David had reached a turning point. Their love had grown stronger, their bond unshakable, but they knew that staying in their small town would always mean navigating a landscape of judgment and fear. It was a realization that both frightened and emboldened them, setting the stage for the next chapter of their journey.

Chapter 5: Shadows of Small-Town Life

Ryan and David soon realized that their growing love couldn't be confined to stolen moments and still places. Living openly in their small, conservative town came with challenges they hadn't fully anticipated. The whispers and judgmental stares that followed them were more than a nuisance—they were a reminder of the societal pressures that sought to define them.

Their first public outing as a couple was a modest one: a peaceful dinner at the town's only Italian restaurant. The plan was simple—to enjoy a meal and leave quietly. But even in the dimly lit dining room, where they sat at a corner table, their presence didn't go unnoticed. Conversations seemed to falter as they walked in, and several patrons cast furtive glances their way.

Ryan shifted uncomfortably in his seat. "Maybe we should've just ordered takeout."

David reached across the table, his hand brushing Ryan's in a subtle but reassuring gesture. "No. We deserve to be here as much as anyone else."

Despite David's words, the tension lingered. The waiter's forced politeness, the hushed murmurs from nearby tables, and the pointed stares from an older couple a few seats away all added to the weight pressing down on them. By the time their food arrived, Ryan's appetite had all but vanished.
"I hate this," Ryan muttered, pushing a piece of lasagna around his plate. "I hate feeling like we're on display."

David sighed, his own frustration evident. "I know. But if we keep hiding, they win."

The small-town scrutiny extended beyond public outings. At work, Ryan noticed a shift in how some of his coworkers interacted with him. Conversations that once flowed easily were now tinged with awkward pauses and uncomfortable silences. Meanwhile, David, who worked in a nearby office, found himself the subject of rumors that seemed to spread faster than wildfire.

"Did you hear what Marcy said?" David asked one evening, tossing his bag onto the couch as he recounted his day.

Ryan frowned. "What now?"

"She told the receptionist I'm 'confused' and going through a phase." David rolled his eyes, but his tone betrayed the sting of the comment. "As if she knows anything about my life."

Ryan sat beside him, placing a comforting hand on his shoulder. "People talk because they don't understand. It's easier for them to judge than to question their own beliefs."

David leaned into Ryan's touch, grateful for the support. "It's exhausting, though. Sometimes I feel like it'd just be easier to move somewhere no one knows us."

The idea of leaving their hometown was a recurring topic in their conversations. Both Ryan and David felt the pull of a fresh start, a chance to build a life free from the constraints of small-town prejudice. But the thought of leaving behind everything they had ever known—family, friends, and the familiarity of their surroundings—was daunting.

One evening, as they sat on the porch of Ryan's childhood home, David voiced what they had both been thinking.

"We can't keep living like this," he said, staring out at the darkened street. "It's like we're constantly walking on eggshells, waiting for someone to push us back into the shadows."
Ryan nodded, his gaze fixed on the stars above. "But leaving means starting over. Finding new jobs, new friends, a new place to live… It's a lot."

"It is," David agreed. "But isn't it worth it if it means we can finally live without fear?"

Ryan turned to him, the sincerity in David's eyes cutting through his doubts. "Yeah. It is."

Their decision to leave wasn't made lightly. They spent weeks weighing their options, researching cities that were known for their inclusivity and opportunities. Los Angeles quickly emerged as the top contender—a sprawling metropolis where diversity was celebrated, and anonymity was possible.

The practicalities of the move were overwhelming. Ryan and David spent countless evenings poring over job listings, apartment rentals, and moving expenses. But amidst the stress, there was an underlying excitement—a sense of hope that buoyed them through the challenges.

"I found a place," David announced one night, holding up his laptop. "It's small, but it's close to downtown, and the landlord seems friendly."

Ryan leaned over to look at the listing, a smile tugging at his lips. "It's perfect."

The hardest part of their decision was telling their families. Both Ryan and David were close to their parents, and the thought of leaving them behind weighed heavily on their hearts. When they finally broke the news over Sunday dinner at Ryan's mom's house, the room fell silent.

"You're really leaving?" Ryan's mom asked, her voice tinged with both sadness and understanding.

Ryan nodded. "We need this, Mom. We need a chance to live our lives without… all of this."

Her eyes glistened with unshed tears, but she managed a smile. "I understand. And I'm proud of you. Both of you."

David's parents were equally supportive, though his father's lingering silence spoke to the difficulty of letting his son go. "It's hard to see you leave," his father finally said, his voice gruff. "But I get it. And I'm proud of you too."

Their final weeks in the town were bittersweet. They spent their days packing up their belongings, saying goodbye to friends, and revisiting places that held memories of their childhood. Each farewell was a reminder of what they were leaving behind, but it was also a testament to the strength of their love and their determination to build a future together.

On their last night in town, Ryan and David returned to the park where they had spent so many evenings. Sitting on their favorite bench, they held hands and watched the sun dip below the horizon, painting the sky in hues of gold and crimson.

"This is it," Ryan said, his voice a mix of excitement and nervousness.

David squeezed his hand, his smile steady and reassuring. "This is just the beginning."

As the stars emerged one by one, they sat in silence, the weight of their decision giving way to a sense of hope.

They didn't know what awaited them in Los Angeles, but they knew they would face it together. And that, they realized, was all that mattered

Chapter 6: A Leap of Faith

Ryan and David stood side by side, their car packed to the brim with everything they owned, a mix of practical essentials and sentimental keepsakes. The moving truck they'd rented idled nearby, its presence a tangible reminder of the monumental change they were about to embrace. The quiet street outside Ryan's childhood home seemed to hold its breath, as though marking the gravity of the moment.

"You ready for this?" David asked, his voice steady but laced with emotion.

Ryan nodded, his eyes scanning the familiar landscape of the town he'd called home for so long. "As ready as I'll ever be."

Their families stood gathered on the sidewalk, offering final hugs, words of encouragement, and a few tearful goodbyes. Ryan's mom clung to him a little longer than usual, her voice soft as she whispered, "Go live your life, sweetheart. I'm so proud of you."

David's mother, always the practical one, pressed a neatly folded envelope into his hand. "Just in case you need a little extra," she said with a small smile. "And don't forget to call."

The goodbye was harder than either of them had anticipated, but as they drove away from the town limits, the weight of their decision was offset by the thrill of what lay ahead. The open road stretched before them, a symbol of possibility and freedom.

The drive to Los Angeles was long, but it became a journey of reflection and bonding. They took turns driving, the miles passing in a blur of laughter, shared playlists, and serene moments of introspection. At night, they stayed in modest motels, their conversations stretching late into the evening as they planned for their new life together.

"I've always wanted to live somewhere I could just…

blend in," Ryan mused one evening as they sat on the bed, sharing takeout from a nearby diner. "Somewhere I wouldn't feel like every move I made was being judged."

David nodded, his gaze thoughtful. "Me too. I think LA could be that place for us. A place where we can just be ourselves."

Their excitement was tempered by moments of doubt— what if they didn't find jobs right away? What if the city was too overwhelming? But every time those fears surfaced, they reminded each other of why they were doing this.
"We've made it this far," David said during one particularly tense moment, when the GPS had rerouted them down a confusing series of side roads. "We'll figure it out."

Ryan smiled, his tension easing. "Yeah. Together."

When they finally arrived in Los Angeles, the city

greeted them with its sprawling skyline, palm-lined streets, and the kind of vibrant energy that seemed to hum in the air. Their apartment, while small, felt like a palace compared to the cramped motels they'd stayed in along the way. The walls were bare, the furniture minimal, but it was theirs—a blank canvas for the life they were about to build.

As they unpacked, they marveled at the diversity of their new neighborhood. The street outside was a tapestry of cultures, with a mix of bustling shops, colorful murals, and the enticing aromas of international cuisine wafting from nearby restaurants. For the first time in years, they felt a sense of anonymity, a freedom to explore their identities without the constant scrutiny of others.

Their first night in the apartment was spent on a makeshift bed of blankets and pillows, the furniture still in transit. They lay side by side, the glow of the city lights filtering through the windows and talked about their hopes and dreams.

"I want this to be a fresh start," Ryan said, his voice low but firm. "A place where we can really figure out who we are."

David reached for his hand, squeezing it gently. "It will be. We'll make it one."

Adjusting to life in Los Angeles was both exciting and overwhelming. The city was a whirlwind of activity, a stark contrast to the slow pace of their hometown. There were new streets to navigate, new routines to establish, and new opportunities to pursue.

David quickly found a job at a marketing agency, his charm and creativity earning him a position on their team. Ryan, who had always been more reserved, took longer to find his footing, eventually landing a position at a local nonprofit that focused on community outreach.

"I love what they stand for," Ryan told David one evening after his first day. "It feels good to be part of something that's making a difference.

David smiled, proud of Ryan's determination. "You're going to be amazing there. I know it."

In their free time, they explored the city, marveling at its diversity and energy. They strolled along Venice Beach, wandered through the art galleries of Downtown LA, and attended their first LGBTQ+ pride event, where they found themselves surrounded by a vibrant and supportive community.

The pride event was a revelation for both of them. For the first time, they felt like they belonged—like they were part of something bigger than themselves. The sea of rainbow flags, the smiles of strangers, and the shared stories of resilience and love all reinforced their belief that they had made the right choice in coming here.

"I've never felt this… free," Ryan admitted as they stood in the middle of the bustling crowd, their hands intertwined.

David nodded, his expression soft. "Me neither. This is where we're meant to be."

As the weeks turned into months, their apartment began to feel like home. They hung pictures on the walls, filled the shelves with books and mementos, and hosted small gatherings for the friends they were beginning to make. The initial struggles of settling into a new city faded into the background, replaced by a sense of purpose and belonging.

One evening, as they sat on their tiny balcony overlooking the city, David turned to Ryan with a smile. "We did it," he said simply. "We took the leap."

Ryan smiled back, his heart full. "And I wouldn't change a thing."

Their move to Los Angeles wasn't just a change of scenery—it was a declaration of love, resilience, and hope. It was the beginning of a new chapter, one that promised endless possibilities and a chance to live authentically. And for Ryan and David, that was more than enough.

Chapter 7: Love in the City

Los Angeles was unlike anything Ryan and David had ever known. The city teemed with life at all hours, a kaleidoscope of diversity and culture that felt both overwhelming and exhilarating. In their hometown, difference had been a source of scrutiny, here, it was celebrated. For the first time, Ryan and David felt a sense of belonging—not just in their relationship, but within a community that welcomed them with open arms.

Their new neighborhood quickly became their haven. The streets buzzed with the hum of people, food trucks lined the curbs, and street performers filled the air with music. Each morning, they would grab coffee from a corner café where the barista always remembered their order, and on weekends, they'd explore local farmers' markets, hand in hand.

"This feels like home," Ryan said one Saturday as they

strolled through a bustling market, the scent of fresh flowers and baked goods filling the air. He held a bouquet of sunflowers that David had insisted on buying for him.

David smiled, brushing his hand against Ryan's. "That's because we're building it together."
The LGBTQ+ community in Los Angeles became an anchor for them. Through local events and meetups, they found themselves surrounded by people who shared their experiences and offered unwavering support. One of their first connections was with a couple named Alex and Miguel, who had been together for over a decade.

"You'll love it here," Alex said during their first dinner together. They had invited Ryan and David to their apartment, a cozy space adorned with travel photos and pride flags. "The city isn't perfect, but it gives you the space to be yourself."

Miguel nodded. "And the community here is incredible. There's always someone willing to lend an ear or a hand."

The friendship with Alex and Miguel grew quickly, and through them, Ryan and David were introduced to an even larger network of friends. Barbecues, game nights, and volunteer events became regular occurrences, each one reinforcing the sense of family they had begun to build.

As their social circle expanded, so did their confidence in living openly. They attended their first pride parade, an event that was as vibrant and affirming as it was emotional. The streets were alive with color, music, and joy, a celebration of love in all its forms.

Ryan found himself overwhelmed by the sheer scale of it. Standing amidst a sea of rainbow flags and smiling faces, he felt a swell of pride and acceptance he hadn't known was possible. David noticed the tears welling up in Ryan's eyes and pulled him into a tight hug.

"Can you believe this?" Ryan asked, his voice thick with emotion. "This is what freedom feels like."

David nodded, his own eyes glistening. "We're exactly where we're supposed to be."

The parade became a turning point for them. It wasn't just about celebrating who they were—it was about recognizing the courage it had taken to get there and the love that had carried them through.

Their relationship deepened in ways neither of them had anticipated. The freedom to love openly brought out new layers of intimacy and understanding. They discovered the joy of small, everyday moments: cooking dinner together in their tiny kitchen, binge-watching shows on lazy Sundays, and leaving each other notes on the bathroom mirror.

One evening, as they walked along Santa Monica Pier, the sound of waves crashing against the shore, David paused and turned to Ryan.

"Do you ever think about what's next for us?" he asked, his tone thoughtful.

Ryan tilted his head. "What do you mean?"

"I mean… where we're going. What we're building together."

Ryan smiled, the answer coming easily. "I think we're already building it. One day at a time."

Their love blossomed in the vibrant energy of the city, but it wasn't without its challenges. The fast pace of life and the pressures of their new jobs occasionally left them drained and irritable. Arguments would flare over seemingly trivial matters—whose turn it was to take out the trash, or how David always left his shoes in the hallway.

But even in their disagreements, there was a commitment to each other that never wavered. They learned to communicate more openly, to apologize when they were wrong, and to prioritize their relationship above all else.

"We're not perfect," David said one night after an argument had cooled. "But I think that's what makes this real."

Ryan nodded, reaching for David's hand. "As long as we're in it together, we'll figure it out."

In time, their love story became a testament to the resilience of the human spirit. They celebrated their commitment with a small wedding ceremony, surrounded by their closest friends and their families, who had flown in from their hometown. The event was held in a sunlit garden, the air filled with laughter, music, and the scent of blooming flowers.

Ryan and David wrote their own vows, each one a heartfelt declaration of love and gratitude. As they stood before their gathered loved ones, their hands clasped tightly together, there was no doubt that they had found something extraordinary.

"I promise to love you for who you are, and for who you will become," David said, his voice steady despite the emotion in his eyes. "To stand by your side, no matter what life throws at us."

Ryan smiled, his heart full. "And I promise to do the same. To choose you, every day, for the rest of our lives."

The ceremony was followed by a reception that was as lively and joyful as the city they now called home. As they danced beneath a canopy of twinkling lights, surrounded by their chosen family, Ryan and David felt a profound sense of peace.

They had taken a leap of faith, and it had brought them here—to a life filled with love, community, and the promise of a future they were building together.

Chapter 8: Battling the Demons Within

Life in Los Angeles had given Ryan and David a fresh start, but it also unearthed challenges they had yet to fully confront. Amid the vibrant energy of the city and the joy of building a life together, there were shadows that lingered—shadows that Ryan, in particular, had spent years trying to keep at bay.

Ryan had always been aware of the emotional highs and lows that marked his days, but in the past, he had dismissed them as part of life's natural rhythm. Yet, as the months passed, the swings became harder to ignore. Some days, he felt invincible, tackling tasks with a boundless energy that left David in awe. Other days, he struggled to get out of bed, consumed by a heaviness he couldn't explain.

One evening, after a particularly tough day, Ryan sat on the couch, staring blankly at the wall. David entered the room, carrying two mugs of tea, and immediately noticed the tension in Ryan's posture.

"Hey," David said gently, setting the mugs on the coffee table. "You've been quiet today. Want to talk about it?" Ryan hesitated, his hands fidgeting in his lap. "I don't know," he admitted. "I just… feel off. Like there's this weight I can't shake."

David sat beside him, his expression filled with concern. "This isn't the first time you've felt this way, is it?" Ryan shook his head. "No. But it's been getting worse."

David's concern for Ryan grew over the following weeks as the cycles of highs and lows continued. While Ryan excelled at his nonprofit job on his good days, his bad days left him drained and withdrawn. It wasn't just mood swings—it was a deep struggle that affected every aspect of his life.

One night, after Ryan had gone to bed early, David stayed up researching. The more he read about mood disorders, the more he recognized the patterns in Ryan's behavior. By the time he turned off his laptop, he had resolved to broach the subject with Ryan in the morning.

Over breakfast the next day, David gently brought it up. "I've been thinking about what you've been going through," he said, his tone careful. "And I think it might be time to talk to someone—a professional, I mean." Ryan frowned, his initial instinct to brush off the suggestion. "You think I need therapy?"

"I think we both do, honestly," David said with a small smile. "But for you… I think it could help to get some clarity on what's been happening. It doesn't mean there's something wrong with you. It just means you're human."

Ryan studied David's face, searching for any trace of judgment but finding only love. After a moment, he sighed and nodded. "Okay. Let's look into it."

The decision to seek help marked a turning point in their relationship. Ryan's first therapy appointment was nerve-wracking, but David supported him every step of the way, waiting outside the office during the sessions and encouraging him to share his thoughts afterward.

Through therapy, Ryan was diagnosed with bipolar disorder, a revelation that brought both relief and fear. On one hand, it gave a name to the struggles he had faced for years, on the other, it forced him to confront the reality of living with a mental health condition.

"I feel broken," Ryan admitted one evening as they sat on their balcony, the city lights twinkling below. "Like I'm too much to handle."

David reached for his hand, his grip firm and steady. "You're not broken, Ryan. You're just… complex. And I'm not going anywhere."

Ryan's journey toward understanding and managing his bipolar disorder was a learning process for both of them. Therapy became a regular part of his routine, and he began exploring medication options with the help of his

psychiatrist. There were trial-and-error periods, with side effects and adjustments that tested his patience, but Ryan remained committed to finding balance.
54

David, meanwhile, threw himself into learning about bipolar disorder, attending support groups and reading everything he could find. He wanted to be the partner Ryan deserved, someone who could walk beside him without minimizing or overshadowing his experience.

"I'm proud of you," Ryan told David one evening as they cooked dinner together. "For how much you're doing to support me. I don't think I say that enough."

David smiled, his hand resting briefly on Ryan's shoulder. "I'm just doing what anyone who loves you would do. We're in this together."
Despite the progress they were making, there were still tough days. Episodes of mania would leave Ryan restless and impulsive, while depressive periods made him feel like a burden. Arguments occasionally flared, fueled by the strain of navigating such uncharted territory.

One particularly difficult evening, after an argument about finances, Ryan broke down. "I'm sorry," he said, tears streaming down his face. "I'm trying, but sometimes it feels like I'm dragging you down with me."

David knelt beside him, his hands framing Ryan's face. "You're not dragging me down," he said firmly. "We're lifting each other up. And we'll keep doing it, no matter how hard it gets."

Over time, they began to find a rhythm. Therapy and medication helped Ryan manage his symptoms, while open communication strengthened their bond. They learned to celebrate small victories, like a week without a depressive episode or a productive therapy session. And on the tough days, they reminded each other that progress wasn't linear, but it was still progress. Their network of friends in Los Angeles also became a vital source of support. Alex and Miguel, who had experienced their own challenges with mental health, offered guidance and understanding. "You're not alone," Alex told Ryan during one of their game nights. "And you're stronger than you think."

Ryan's battle with bipolar disorder became a defining part of their relationship, but it didn't define him. With David by his side, he discovered a resilience he hadn't known he possessed. Together, they faced the ups and downs with courage and compassion, knowing that their love was a steady anchor in the storm.

And as they sat together one evening, watching the sunset paint the sky in hues of gold and pink, Ryan turned to David with a small smile. "Thank you," he said simply. "For everything."

David leaned in, pressing a kiss to Ryan's temple. "Always."

Chapter 9: Healing Hearts

The journey toward healing was not linear. While Ryan made strides in therapy and found a medication regimen that helped stabilize his mood, there were still days when the weight of his bipolar disorder felt insurmountable. But what became clear to both him and David was that healing wasn't a solitary act—it was a shared endeavor, built on patience, understanding, and unwavering support.

David became Ryan's anchor during moments of turmoil. When Ryan woke in the middle of the night, his mind racing with anxious thoughts, David would sit with him on the couch, rubbing soothing circles on his back as they talked through his fears. On the days when Ryan couldn't find the motivation to leave bed, David would bring him a cup of tea, climb in beside him, and remind him that it was okay to rest.

"Some days are harder than others," Ryan admitted during one of their late-night conversations. "But knowing you're here… it makes the hard days a little easier."

David smiled, his hand squeezing Ryan's. "That's because we're a team. Whatever you're facing, I'm facing it with you."

To further support Ryan's healing, the couple began incorporating mindfulness practices into their daily routine. It started with a suggestion from Ryan's therapist: a simple meditation app that guided them through breathing exercises each morning. While David had initially been skeptical—"Do we really just sit here and breathe?"—he quickly saw the benefits for both of them.

"I feel… calmer," David admitted after one of their sessions. "More focused. Maybe there's something to this after all."

Ryan chuckled, his smile soft. "Told you it was worth a try."

They also found solace in activities that allowed them to reconnect with the present moment. Long walks through Griffith Park became a weekend ritual, the rustle of leaves and the chirping of birds providing a soothing backdrop to their conversations. Cooking together took on a new significance as they experimented with recipes that nourished both their bodies and minds.

As Ryan's healing progressed, their relationship deepened in unexpected ways. Vulnerability had always been a cornerstone of their bond, but now, it became a source of strength. They learned to communicate more openly about their needs and boundaries, creating a space where both felt seen and heard.

One evening, as they sat on their balcony watching the city lights twinkle below, Ryan turned to David with a thoughtful expression. "Do you ever worry about the future?" he asked. "About what happens if my bipolar disorder gets worse?"

David was still for a moment, his gaze steady. "I think about it," he admitted. "But I also know that we'll face it together, just like we've faced everything else. You're not your disorder, Ryan. You're so much more than that."

Ryan's eyes filled with tears, his heart swelling with gratitude. "You always know what to say."

"That's because I love you," David replied simply. "And I always will."

The support they received from their friends and the LGBTQ+ community in Los Angeles became another vital part of their healing journey. Alex and Miguel, who had faced their own challenges with mental health, were always there to lend an ear or offer advice. They invited Ryan and David to join a local support group, where they connected with others who understood their struggles.

"It helps to know we're not alone," Ryan said after their first meeting, his voice tinged with relief. "Hearing other people's stories… it's like seeing a piece of yourself in someone else."

David nodded, his hand resting lightly on Ryan's shoulder. "We're all stronger together."

Through therapy, mindfulness, and the unwavering support of those around them, Ryan began to rebuild his sense of self. He discovered new passions, like journaling and photography, that allowed him to channel his emotions into something tangible. David encouraged these pursuits, often joining Ryan on spontaneous photo walks through the city.

"You've got an eye for this," David remarked one afternoon as Ryan snapped a picture of a mural. "Maybe you should think about doing it professionally."

Ryan laughed, shaking his head. "Let's not get ahead of ourselves. For now, I'm just enjoying it."

"That's what matters," David said, his smile warm. "As long as it makes you happy."

Healing didn't erase the challenges they faced, but it gave them the tools to navigate them with resilience and grace. They learned to celebrate the small victories—a week without a depressive episode, a productive therapy session, or a day when Ryan felt truly at peace.

On one particularly calm evening, as they sat together watching a movie, Ryan turned to David and said, "I don't know where I'd be without you."

David smiled, pulling Ryan closer. "You'd still be the amazing person you are. I just get to remind you of that."

Their journey toward healing was far from over, but they knew they were on the right path. Together, they were building a life that wasn't defined by struggle but by love, growth, and the unwavering belief that they could face anything as long as they had each other.

Chapter 10: Finding Community

As Ryan and David settled further into their life in Los Angeles, they found themselves drawn deeper into the city's vibrant LGBTQ+ community. What began as casual outings to local events turned into meaningful connections, a web of friendships that supported them through every twist and turn of their journey.

It was Alex and Miguel who first introduced them to the broader network. "You've got to come to the next potluck," Alex insisted one evening as they gathered for a relaxing dinner. "It's not just about the food—it's about the people. Everyone's got a story, and you'll feel right at home."

The potluck, held in a cozy backyard adorned with string lights and mismatched chairs, turned out to be exactly as Alex had promised. Dozens of people mingled, sharing laughter, stories, and an impressive array of dishes. Ryan and David felt an instant sense of belonging, their initial nervousness fading with each conversation.

"Your story is incredible," said Sam, a trans woman who had recently moved to Los Angeles herself. "It takes so much courage to leave everything behind and start over."

Ryan smiled, his heart warming at her words. "It hasn't been easy, but it's been worth it."

David nodded beside him. "And it's people like you who make it feel even more worth it."
Through these gatherings, Ryan and David began to see the transformative power of community. The support they received wasn't just emotional—it was practical, too. When Ryan mentioned his interest in photography, a friend named Jamie offered to connect him with a local studio that was looking for part-time assistants.

"It's a great way to get your foot in the door," Jamie said. "And who knows? You might even love it."

David found his own avenues of connection,

volunteering at a community center that provided resources for LGBTQ+ youth. "They remind me of us," he told Ryan after his first week. "Scared, uncertain, but full of potential. It feels good to help them find their footing."

Ryan couldn't help but beam with pride. "You're doing something amazing, David. You're changing lives."

Their newfound sense of community also brought opportunities for advocacy. Ryan and David began participating in pride marches, charity events, and panels that raised awareness about mental health and LGBTQ+ issues. Their story, once something they had kept private, became a source of inspiration for others.

At one event, a young man approached them with tears in his eyes. "I've been struggling with my mental health," he admitted. "Hearing you speak about your journey… it gives me hope."

Ryan was momentarily speechless, his heart aching with

empathy. "You're not alone," he said, his voice steady. "There's a whole community here ready to support you. And you're stronger than you realize."

David placed a reassuring hand on the young man's shoulder. "Just take it one day at a time. And don't be afraid to reach out."

The connections they formed weren't limited to large events. Their group of friends became like an extended family, sharing in their triumphs and supporting them through their challenges. When Ryan celebrated his one-year anniversary of starting therapy, they hosted a small gathering to mark the milestone.

"It's not just about me," Ryan said as they raised their glasses. "It's about all of you. You've shown me what it means to be part of something bigger, and I'm so grateful for that."

David smiled, his heart full as he clinked his glass against Ryan's. "Here's to community," he said. "And to the incredible people who make it feel like home."

For Ryan and David, finding community wasn't just about belonging—it was about growth. It gave them the courage to embrace their identities, the strength to face life's challenges, and the joy of knowing they were never truly alone. Together, they had built a network of love and support that would carry them forward, no matter what lay ahead.

Chapter 11: A Glimpse of Happiness

Ryan and David's life in Los Angeles was beginning to feel like a mosaic of joy, resilience, and newfound freedom. With every step forward, they pieced together moments that felt like glimpses of pure happiness—moments that reminded them of why they had taken the leap to begin with.

The city's vibrant energy became their playground. On weekends, they explored its cultural offerings, from art galleries and theater productions to the quirky street performances of Venice Beach. Ryan, camera in hand, often paused to capture these scenes, his photographs gradually forming a portfolio that spoke to the beauty of their new life.

"Look at this one," Ryan said one afternoon, showing David a black-and-white photo he had taken of a street musician lost in his music. The intensity of the man's expression seemed to leap off the screen.

David studied the image, a smile spreading across his face. "You've got a gift, you know that? You see the world in a way most people don't."

Ryan blushed, brushing off the compliment. "I just like telling stories through pictures."

"And you do it beautifully," David said firmly. "You should share these with more people."

One of their favorite escapes became the beaches of Malibu, where they spent hours walking along the shore, their feet sinking into the cool sand as waves lapped at their ankles. The rhythmic sound of the ocean seemed to wash away the stresses of their daily lives, leaving them free to simply be.

On one such evening, as the sun dipped below the horizon, painting the sky in shades of orange and pink, Ryan turned to David with a thoughtful expression. "Do you ever stop and think about how far we've come?"

David smiled, his gaze fixed on the horizon. "All the time. It feels surreal sometimes, doesn't it? Like we're living a life we used to only dream about."

Ryan nodded, his heart swelling with gratitude. "I'm just glad we're living it together."

David reached for Ryan's hand, their fingers intertwining. "Me too. Always."

The joy of their life together wasn't limited to grand adventures. It was also found in the calm, everyday moments that filled their home with warmth. Cooking dinner together became a ritual, with music playing softly in the background as they danced around the kitchen. Ryan would often laugh as David dramatically lip-synced to their favorite songs, his antics never failing to brighten the room.

One evening, as they shared a simple meal of pasta and wine, Ryan leaned back in his chair and smiled. "You know what my favorite part of all this is?"

David raised an eyebrow, a playful grin on his face. "The pasta?"

Ryan laughed, shaking his head. "No. It's this. Just… being here with you. It doesn't matter what we're doing—it just feels right."

David's grin softened into a tender smile. "That's because it is right."

Their happiness wasn't without its challenges, but they had learned to navigate life's hurdles with grace and humor. When Ryan's photography gig turned into a full-time opportunity, he found himself juggling deadlines and creative blocks. David, who was thriving in his work at the community center, offered constant encouragement, reminding Ryan to take breaks and prioritize self-care.

"You're not a machine," David said one evening when he found Ryan hunched over his laptop, editing photos for an upcoming exhibit. "Come on, let's take a walk.

The work will still be here when you get back."

Ryan sighed but allowed himself to be pulled away from the screen. As they strolled through their neighborhood, the cool night air refreshing his mind, he realized how much he needed these moments of pause.

"Thanks for always looking out for me," Ryan said, leaning into David as they walked.

"That's what I'm here for," David replied, his arm wrapping around Ryan's shoulders.

Their journey was also marked by celebrations— birthdays, anniversaries, and milestones that they cherished deeply. For their first anniversary in Los Angeles, David planned a surprise picnic under the stars at Griffith Observatory. He had packed Ryan's favorite foods and brought along a blanket, the city lights twinkling below them as they toasted to the life they had built together.

"I can't believe you did all this," Ryan said, his voice filled with emotion. "It's perfect."

David smiled, his eyes shining with love. "You're perfect."

These glimpses of happiness became the foundation of their relationship, a reminder that even amidst life's challenges, there was always joyed to be found. They weren't just surviving—they were thriving, creating a life filled with love, laughter, and an unwavering commitment to each other.

As they lay in bed one night, the city still around them, Ryan whispered, "I never knew life could feel this full."

David smiled, his hand resting over Ryan's. "That's because we're living it together."

Chapter 12: A Mother's Love

Life in Los Angeles had given Ryan and David a sense of belonging they'd never experienced before, but even the excitement of their new life couldn't prepare them for the phone call that would change everything. Late one evening, as David was cleaning up after dinner, his phone buzzed on the counter. It was his sister.

The urgency in her voice was unmistakable. "Mom's not doing well, David," she said, her words heavy with emotion. "The doctors think it's time to start making arrangements."

David's hand tightened around the phone, his heart sinking. "I'll be there as soon as I can."

When he hung up, Ryan was already by his side. "What's going on?" he asked, concern etched across his face.

David swallowed hard, struggling to find the words. "It's my mom. She's… not doing well. I need to go home."

Ryan nodded without hesitation. "We'll go together."

The drive back to Georgia was somber, the miles stretching endlessly as David wrestled with a mix of emotions. Ryan kept one hand on the wheel and the other resting on David's knee, offering silent support. They stopped only, when necessary, both of them eager to reach David's hometown.
When they arrived, David's mother was in her room, her frail body propped up on pillows. The years had taken their toll, but her eyes still sparkled with the warmth and wisdom David had always admired.

"My boy," she said softly as David entered the room, her voice weak but filled with love.

David knelt beside her bed, taking her hand in his. "I'm here, Mom."

She smiled faintly, her gaze shifting to Ryan, who stood quietly in the doorway. "And you brought your other half," she said with a knowing look. "Come closer, Ryan."

Ryan hesitated for a moment before stepping forward. He had met David's mother only a handful of times, but her kindness had always stood out. Now, seeing her in this state, his heart ached for both her and David.

"You take care of him, you hear?" she said, her voice firm despite her condition.
Ryan nodded, his throat tightening. "I will."

The days that followed were a blur of family gatherings, whispered conversations, and bittersweet memories. David spent every moment he could by his mother's side, sharing stories and holding her hand. Ryan stayed in the background, offering loving support and helping with anything the family needed.

One afternoon, as Ryan and David sat on the porch,

David turned to Ryan with tears in his eyes. "I don't know how I'm going to do this," he admitted. "How do you say goodbye to someone who's been your whole world?"

Ryan reached for David's hand, his grip steady. "You don't have to say goodbye," he said softly. "You carry her with you. In your heart, in your memories, in everything she's taught you. She'll always be a part of you."

David nodded, his tears falling freely now. "I don't know what I'd do without you."

"You'll never have to find out," Ryan replied, his voice resolute.

As the weeks went on, the inevitable happened. David's mother passed peacefully, surrounded by her family. The funeral was a small, intimate affair, filled with laughter, tears, and stories that celebrated her life. David delivered a heartfelt eulogy, his voice trembling but steady as he spoke of the love and strength his mother had given him.

"She taught me to be kind, to be brave, and to always stand by the people I love," he said, his gaze briefly meeting Ryan's. "And I'll carry those lessons with me for the rest of my life."

After the funeral, Ryan and David stayed in Georgia for a while, helping David's family sort through his mother's belongings and manage the practicalities of her passing. It was a time of healing and reflection, one that brought David closer to his siblings and allowed Ryan to see a new side of the man he loved.

One evening, as they sat in the living room going through old photo albums, David found a picture of himself as a child, sitting on his mother's lap. He stared at it for a long moment before showing it to Ryan.

"She was my first home," David said quietly. "And now… you're my home."

Ryan leaned over, kissing David's temple. "We'll carry her with us, always."

Returning to Los Angeles felt like stepping into a new chapter. The grief was still there, but so was a sense of gratitude—for the time they had shared with David's mother, and for the love that had carried them through.

As they unpacked their bags and settled back into their routine, Ryan turned to David with a small smile. "You okay?"

David nodded, his eyes soft. "Yeah. I think I am."
And as they sat together that evening, the city lights twinkling outside their window, they held each other close, knowing that love—both the kind they'd lost and the kind they still shared—would always be their greatest strength.

Chapter 13: Embracing Family

Returning to Los Angeles brought a sense of relief, but it also left David grappling with the reality of his loss. His mother's passing had stirred something in him—a need to reconnect not just with her memory, but also with the broader concept of family. For years, his relationships with his siblings had been cordial but distant. Now, he felt a deep desire to bridge the gaps and strengthen those bonds.

Ryan supported David wholeheartedly. "Family isn't just the people you're born into," Ryan reminded him one evening as they sat together on their balcony. "It's the people you choose, too. And it's never too late to strengthen those connections."

David nodded, his expression thoughtful. "You're right. And I think… I think it's time I really tried."

Over the next few months, David made an effort to reach

out to his siblings. He started with phone calls—simple check-ins that gradually turned into longer conversations filled with laughter, shared memories, and updates on their lives. His sister, who had been his closest confidante growing up, became a regular presence in his life again.

"I forgot how much I missed this," David admitted after a particularly long call with his brother. "It's like we're finally seeing each other as adults, not just as kids who fought over the TV remote."

Ryan smiled, resting a hand on David's shoulder. "It's amazing what a little effort can do. And I'm proud of you for taking the first step."

Reconnecting with family wasn't always easy. There were moments of tension, especially when old wounds resurfaced. One of David's brothers had struggled to accept David's sexuality in the past, and while their interactions were civil, there was still an underlying unease.

During a family video call, the brother made an offhand comment that caused the conversation to falter. "You've really settled into that LA lifestyle, haven't you?" he said, his tone clipped.

David tensed, his jaw tightening. Ryan, who was sitting beside him, gave his hand a reassuring squeeze.

"I have," David said evenly. "And I'm happier than I've ever been. I hope you can be happy for me, too."
The silence that followed was heavy, but eventually, his brother nodded. "I'm trying, David," he said quietly. "I really am."

It wasn't a resolution, but it was a start.

Meanwhile, Ryan found himself reflecting on his own family dynamics. As an only child, his family connections had always revolved around his mother and grandmother. While they had been loving and supportive, Ryan realized he had never fully opened up to them about his struggles or his relationship with

David.

During one of their weekly phone calls, Ryan decided to change that. "Mom, can I talk to you about something?" he began, his voice steady but nervous.

"Of course, sweetheart," his mother replied, her tone warm.

Ryan took a deep breath. "I've been dealing with some mental health challenges—bipolar disorder, to be specific. And David… he's been my rock through all of it."

There was a pause on the other end of the line, and Ryan braced himself for her response.
"Oh, honey," his mother said softly. "Why didn't you tell me sooner? I'm so proud of you—for facing this, for being honest, and for finding someone like David to stand by you."

Ryan felt a wave of relief wash over him. "Thank you,

Mom. That means more than you know."

The process of embracing family—both biological and chosen—became a shared journey for Ryan and David. They invited David's siblings to visit Los Angeles, hosting them in their small but cozy apartment. The visits were filled with laughter, sightseeing, and the kind of candid conversations that strengthened their bonds.

On one such visit, David's sister pulled him aside. "You've changed," she said, her voice tinged with admiration. "You seem… lighter. Happier."

David smiled, his gaze drifting to Ryan, who was in the kitchen chatting with their guests. "I am," he said simply. "And it's because of him."

As they continued to build their own family in Los Angeles, Ryan and David also deepened their ties with their chosen family—the friends who had become like siblings to them. They celebrated milestones together, from birthdays to job promotions, and supported each other through life's ups and downs.

One evening, as they hosted a dinner party for their closest friends, Ryan raised a toast. "To family," he said, his voice filled with gratitude. "The ones we're born into, the ones we choose, and the ones who choose us."

David smiled, his hand resting on Ryan's. "And to the love that holds it all together."

In embracing family—both near and far, old and new—Ryan and David discovered a profound sense of connection and belonging. They realized that family wasn't about perfection or always agreeing, it was about showing up, supporting one another, and creating a space where love could thrive.

As they sat together that night, the hum of conversation and laughter filling their home, Ryan turned to David with a smile. "This feels right," he said simply.

David nodded, his heart full. "It is."

Chapter 14: Unexpected Opportunities

Life in Los Angeles had settled into a comfortable rhythm for Ryan and David. Their days were filled with meaningful work, their evenings spent with friends or exploring the city. But as they grew more rooted in their new life, they couldn't have anticipated the unexpected turn that would ignite their shared passion for history and connection.

It started one sunny Saturday afternoon when they wandered into a small, unassuming antique shop while strolling through a relaxed part of the city. The shop was a treasure trove of history, its shelves brimming with relics from the past: vintage photographs, ornate jewelry, hand-painted ceramics, and well-loved books whose spines told stories of decades gone by.

Ryan was immediately drawn to a wooden chest tucked into a corner. Its surface was worn, its edges rough, but there was something about it that felt alive with history.

"Look at this," he said, beckoning David over. "Imagine the stories this could tell."

David smiled, watching as Ryan carefully opened the chest to reveal a collection of letters tied with a faded ribbon. "It's incredible," David said, his own curiosity piqued. "Stuff like this… it connects us to people we've never met, lives we've never known."

The moment sparked something in both of them—a shared realization that their love for history, and for the connections it fostered, could become something more.

Over dinner that evening, they couldn't stop talking about the antique shop. "What if we started something like that?" Ryan asked, his excitement barely contained. "A place where people can come to explore the past, find something meaningful, and take a piece of it home." David raised an eyebrow, intrigued. "You're serious?"

"Why not?" Ryan said, leaning forward. "We've always talked about wanting to do something together—

something that's ours. This could be it."

David smiled, his mind already racing with possibilities. "It would be a lot of work."

Ryan grinned. "Good thing we're not afraid of hard work."

The idea quickly took root. They began researching what it would take to open their own antique shop, from sourcing inventory to finding a location. It wasn't long before they stumbled upon an old storefront in a vibrant part of the city that seemed perfect for their vision. The building was in need of some love, but its vintage charm spoke to them immediately.

"This is it," David said as they stood outside, imagining the possibilities. "I can see it now—shelves filled with treasures, the smell of old books and polished wood, and people coming in to find pieces of history."

Ryan smiled, his excitement matching David's. "Let's

do it."

Renovating the space became a labor of love. They spent evenings and weekends painting walls, repairing fixtures, and carefully curating their inventory. Friends pitched in, helping them transform the dusty old building into a welcoming haven for history enthusiasts.

Their shop, which they named Timeless Connections, opened to the public on a crisp autumn morning. The response was immediate and overwhelming. Locals and tourists alike were drawn to the shop's unique charm, its shelves lined with everything from vintage cameras to antique furniture.
"This place is amazing," one customer said as she examined a delicate porcelain figurine. "You can feel the stories in here."

Ryan and David beamed, knowing they had created something special.

Running the shop brought them closer together,

highlighting their individual strengths. Ryan's eye for photography translated into stunning displays and marketing materials, while David's knack for storytelling turned every sale into a meaningful exchange.

"Every piece in here has a story," David told a customer one afternoon as he handed her a 1920s locket. "And now, you get to add your own chapter to it."
The customer smiled, clearly moved. "Thank you," she said. "This means so much to me."

Their venture wasn't without its challenges. There were slow weeks when foot traffic was low, moments of doubt about whether they had made the right choice, and the constant juggling act of running a business while maintaining their personal lives. But every time they faced a hurdle, they reminded each other why they had started this journey.
One evening, after a particularly long day at the shop, Ryan sank onto the couch with a sigh. "Do you ever wonder if we bit off more than we can chew?" he asked,

exhaustion evident in his voice.

David sat beside him, handing him a glass of wine. "Sometimes," he admitted. "But then I see the look on someone's face when they find something meaningful here, and I know it's worth it."

Ryan smiled, leaning his head against David's shoulder. "You always know how to make me feel better."

Over time, Timeless Connections became more than just a shop—it became a community hub. They hosted events like historical lectures, art exhibits, and storytelling nights, bringing people together to celebrate the past while creating new memories.

Their success also brought unexpected recognition. A local magazine featured the shop in an article about hidden gems in Los Angeles, and customers began traveling from far and wide to visit.

"I'm so proud of us," Ryan said one evening as they

locked up the shop. "We built this together."
David smiled, wrapping an arm around Ryan's
shoulders. "And it's just the beginning."
92

The shop wasn't just a business—it was a reflection of
their love, their shared passion for connection, and their
commitment to building a life that honored both the past
and the future. As they stood together in the quiet of the
shop one evening, surrounded by the treasures they had
curated, Ryan turned to David with a smile.

"This feels like home," he said softly.

David nodded, his heart full. "Because it is."

Chapter 15: A Journey of Parenthood

The success of Timeless Connections brought a sense of stability and accomplishment to Ryan and David's lives. But as they settled into the rhythm of their business and their relationship, a new longing began to emerge—a desire to expand their family and share their love with someone new.

Parenthood wasn't something they had seriously discussed before, but the idea began to take root during a quiet evening at home. They had just finished dinner and were curled up on the couch, watching a documentary about foster care.

"Do you ever think about having kids?" David asked, his voice soft but curious.

Ryan glanced at him, surprised by the question. "I've thought about it," he admitted. "But I guess I always assumed it wasn't in the cards for us."

David smiled faintly. "Maybe it could be. I mean, we've built this life together—why not share it with someone who needs it?"

The thought lingered between them, both of them turning it over in their minds. The idea of becoming parents was daunting, but it was also exciting. They had so much love to give, and the thought of creating a family filled them with hope.

Their conversations about parenthood became more frequent in the weeks that followed. They researched their options, from adoption to fostering, and reached out to friends who had navigated similar paths.

"It's not easy," said Alex, one of their closest friends, who had adopted a child with Miguel. "But it's the most rewarding thing we've ever done. If it's something you're serious about, you should go for it."

Ryan and David attended informational sessions, filled out endless paperwork, and underwent the rigorous interviews and evaluations required to become adoptive parents. The process was long and often overwhelming, but they leaned on each other every step of the way.

One evening, as they sat together reviewing their adoption profile, Ryan turned to David with a small smile. "This is really happening, isn't it?"

David nodded, his hand resting on Ryan's. "It is. And I can't wait to meet whoever's meant to be a part of our family."

Months later, their dream became a reality. They were matched with a baby girl, just three months old, who had been placed for adoption. The first time they held her, it was as if the world had shifted. She was small and delicate, her dark eyes wide with curiosity as she gazed up at them.

"She's perfect," Ryan whispered, tears streaming down his face.

David nodded, his own eyes glistening. "She's ours."

They named her Hilary, a nod to Ryan's favorite childhood singer, Hilary Duff, and a symbol of hope and joy. From the moment she came into their lives, Hilary filled their home with light and laughter.

Parenthood was a whirlwind of sleepless nights, diaper changes, and countless moments of awe. They quickly discovered the unique challenges of raising a child, but every struggle was worth it.

David took to fatherhood with ease, his natural charm and patience making him a calming presence for Hilary. He would spend hours rocking her to sleep, humming softly as she drifted off in his arms.

Ryan, who had always been the quiet one, found himself stepping into a new role as a father. He loved reading to Hilary, his voice soothing as he introduced her to the magic of stories. Even as an infant, she seemed captivated by his words, her tiny fingers grasping at the pages.

As Hilary grew, so did their bond as a family. Her first steps were met with cheers and laughter, her first words sparking a celebration that brought their friends and family together. Ryan and David documented every milestone, their walls quickly filling with photos and memories.

"She's going to grow up knowing so much love," Ryan said one evening as they watched Hilary toddle around the living room.

David smiled, his arm wrapping around Ryan's shoulders. "Because she's surrounded by it. And because she's got two dads who would do anything for her."

Raising Hilary in Los Angeles presented its own set of challenges. Ryan and David were acutely aware of the societal pressures and prejudices their family might face, but they were determined to create an environment where Hilary felt safe, loved, and empowered.

They made it a priority to expose her to diverse communities and experiences, ensuring she grew up with a strong sense of identity and belonging. They attended family-friendly pride events, enrolled her in inclusive schools, and surrounded her with people who celebrated love in all its forms.

"She's going to be so strong," David said one day as he watched Hilary playing with a group of children at a community event. "She's going to change the world."

Ryan smiled, his heart swelling with pride. "And we're going to be right there beside her."

Parenthood wasn't without its challenges, but it was also filled with immeasurable joy. Every moment, from Hilary's first giggle to her sleepy cuddles at bedtime, reinforced their belief that their family was exactly as it was meant to be.

As they tucked Hilary into bed one night, her tiny hand clutching Ryan's finger, David turned to Ryan with a smile. "We did this," he said softly. "We built this life. This family."

Ryan nodded, his eyes shining. "And I wouldn't trade it for anything."

In Hilary, they found not just a daughter, but a reminder of the love that had brought them together and the life they had worked so hard to create. Together, they were a family—imperfect, resilient, and bound by a love that knew no bounds.

Chapter 16: An Unexpected Twist

Just as life seemed to settle into a joyful rhythm for Ryan, David, and their daughter Hilary, an unexpected twist shook the foundation of their family. It began subtly—small changes in behavior from their teenage son, Devon, whom they had welcomed into their family a few years after adopting Hilary. At first, the signs were easy to dismiss: irritability, slipping grades, and a tendency to withdraw. But as time went on, the changes became harder to ignore.

One evening, as Ryan and David sat in the living room reviewing Hilary's schoolwork, they heard the unmistakable sound of a door slamming. David glanced toward the hallway, his brow furrowing. "That's the third time this week," he murmured.

Ryan set down his coffee cup, his concern evident. "I'll talk to him."

He found Devon in his room, hunched over his desk with

his headphones on. The air was heavy with tension, and Ryan hesitated for a moment before knocking lightly on the doorframe. "Devon? Can we talk?"

Devon didn't respond immediately, but after a moment, he pulled off his headphones and turned to face Ryan. "What?" he asked, his tone sharp.

Ryan sighed, stepping into the room. "I just want to make sure you're okay. You've seemed… different lately."

Devon's eyes flicked away, his jaw tightening. "I'm fine."

But Ryan knew better. There was a guardedness in Devon's demeanor that spoke volumes, and it left Ryan with a sinking feeling that something was deeply wrong.

As weeks turned into months, the tension only grew. Devon's behavior became more erratic—staying out late, missing school, and lying about his whereabouts. When confronted, he became defensive, retreating further into himself. Ryan and David were at a loss, their once open and loving relationship with their son now strained to the breaking point.

"I don't know what to do," David admitted one night as they lay in bed, exhaustion etched across his face. "It feels like he's slipping away from us."

Ryan reached for his hand, his own worry mirrored in his expression. "We can't give up on him. We need to figure out what's going on and how to help."

The truth came to light one night when Devon stumbled through the front door, his speech slurred and his movements unsteady. Ryan and David were immediately at his side, their concern turning to alarm as they realized he was under the influence.

"Devon, what's going on?" David demanded, his voice trembling.

Devon looked at them, his eyes glassy. "It's nothing," he mumbled, brushing past them toward his room.

But it wasn't nothing. In the days that followed, Ryan and David uncovered the extent of Devon's struggles: he had fallen in with the wrong crowd and had been using drugs to cope with feelings of inadequacy and anxiety that he had kept hidden from them.

The revelation was devastating. Ryan and David blamed themselves, wondering if they had missed the signs or failed to provide the support Devon needed. But amidst their guilt and heartbreak, they resolved to do whatever it took to help their son.

The road to recovery was anything but easy. Devon resisted their attempts to intervene at first, lashing out in anger and frustration. "I don't need your help!" he shouted one evening, his voice echoing through the house. "I'm fine on my own!"

But Ryan and David refused to give up. They sought out resources, from addiction counselors to support groups, and surrounded Devon with a network of care. Slowly, he began to let his guard down, opening up about the pressures he had felt to fit in and the pain he had been trying to numb.

"I didn't think I could tell you," Devon admitted one evening during a family counseling session. His voice was quiet, his gaze fixed on the floor. "I didn't want you to be disappointed in me."

Ryan's heart broke at his words. "Devon, we could never be disappointed in you," he said, his voice thick with emotion. "We love you, no matter what."

David nodded, reaching for Devon's hand. "You're not alone in this. We're here, and we're going to get through it together."

The journey through recovery was marked by setbacks and triumphs, moments of despair and glimmers of hope. Devon entered a rehabilitation program, where he worked to address the root causes of his addiction and develop healthier coping mechanisms. Ryan and David attended family therapy sessions, learning how to support Devon without enabling him and rebuilding the trust that had been fractured.

There were days when the progress felt painfully slow, but there were also moments that reminded them of the strength of their family bond. Like the day Devon, freshly out of rehab, joined them for a picnic at the park. For the first time in months, they laughed together, the weight of their struggles momentarily lifting.

"It feels good to be here," Devon said quietly as they sat beneath the shade of a tree, watching Hilary chase butterflies. "With all of you."

Ryan smiled, his heart swelling with gratitude. "It feels good to have you here."

As Devon continued his recovery, he began to discover his own strength and purpose. He joined a support group for teens in recovery and found solace in sharing his story with others. Over time, he became a mentor to younger members, offering them the same hope and encouragement he had received.

Ryan and David couldn't have been prouder. Watching their son transform from a boy lost in pain to a young man determined to overcome his struggles was nothing short of extraordinary.

"You've come so far," David told Devon one evening as they sat on the porch, the warm glow of the sunset casting long shadows across the yard. "And we're so proud of you."

Devon smiled, his gaze steady. "I couldn't have done it without you. Thank you… for not giving up on me."

Ryan reached over, placing a hand on Devon's shoulder. "We never will."

Through the twists and turns of Devon's journey, Ryan and David learned that love wasn't just about celebrating the good times—it was about standing by each other in the darkest moments, fighting for the people they cared about, and believing in the possibility of healing, even when it felt out of reach.

As they sat together that evening, their family whole again, Ryan turned to David with a peaceful smile.

"We've been through so much," he said. "But I think this… this is what makes us stronger."

David nodded, his heart full. "And it's what makes us a family."

Chapter 17: Strength in Unity

The challenges of Devon's recovery taught Ryan and David the true meaning of resilience. Their family had weathered the storm, and while the process had left its scars, it also forged an unbreakable bond between them. Devon's progress was a testament to the love and support they had poured into him, but it was also a reminder of the strength he carried within himself.

As Devon continued his recovery, he started exploring his interests with renewed vigor. Art became his outlet—a way to channel his emotions and express the complexities of his journey. Ryan and David encouraged him every step of the way, helping him set up a small studio space in the corner of their home.

"I didn't know you were so talented," Ryan said one evening as he admired one of Devon's sketches—a detailed portrait of Hilary playing in the garden.

Devon shrugged, a hint of pride in his expression. "It helps me focus. And… it makes me happy."

David smiled, placing a hand on Devon's shoulder. "That's all that matters."

The family's dynamic shifted in beautiful ways. Hilary, now old enough to understand some of what her brother had been through, became a source of light for Devon. She would sit beside him while he painted, chattering away about her day and occasionally offering her own "artistic advice."

"You should add more butterflies," she suggested one afternoon, pointing at a landscape Devon was working on.

Devon chuckled, ruffling her hair. "You think so? Maybe you can help me paint them."

Her face lit up with excitement, and soon, the two of them were collaborating on a colorful masterpiece that quickly earned a spot on the living room wall.

Watching them together, Ryan and David felt a profound

sense of pride. Their family had faced its share of struggles, but moments like this reminded them of the beauty they had created together.

As Devon grew more confident in his abilities, he decided to share his art with a wider audience. With David's encouragement, he entered a local youth art competition. The day of the exhibit, the entire family turned out to support him, their excitement palpable as they walked through the gallery.
"This is amazing," Ryan said, his eyes scanning the rows of artwork. When they reached Devon's piece—a vibrant painting of a phoenix rising from the ashes—both Ryan and David were struck by its depth and power.

"It's… beautiful," David said, his voice thick with emotion. "Just like your journey."

Devon smiled shyly, his eyes glistening. "I couldn't have done it without you."

When Devon's name was announced as one of the

winners, the family erupted in cheers, their pride and joy filling the room.

Beyond their personal triumphs, the family continued to grow their roots in the Los Angeles community. Timeless Connections flourished, becoming a beloved fixture in the neighborhood. Customers often stopped by just to chat with Ryan and David, sharing stories about the items they had purchased and the memories they had created.

One day, a regular customer named Clara approached Ryan with an idea. "You should host a family history day," she suggested. "Invite people to bring in heirlooms and share the stories behind them."

Ryan loved the idea, and after discussing it with David, they decided to make it happen. The event turned out to be a resounding success, with families from all over the city coming to share their histories and connect with one another.

"It's amazing how much we can learn from each other," David said as he watched a young boy showing his grandfather's pocket watch to a captivated audience.

Ryan nodded, his heart full. "It's what this place was meant to be—a space for connection and community."

As the years went on, the family's love for one another only deepened. Hilary grew into a curious and compassionate young girl, eager to learn and explore the world around her. Devon continued to thrive, using his art to inspire others and advocate for mental health awareness.

One evening, as the family gathered around the dinner table, Devon made an announcement. "I've been thinking about going back to school," he said, his voice steady. "To study art therapy."

Ryan and David exchanged a proud glance. "That's an incredible idea," David said. "You'd be amazing at it." Devon smiled, his confidence growing. "I want to help people the way you helped me. To show them that it's possible to heal."

Ryan reached for Devon's hand, his voice filled with emotion. "You're going to make a difference. I know it."

Through every challenge and triumph, Ryan and David's family remained a testament to the power of love, resilience, and unity. They had built a life that honored their past while embracing the future, and they knew that whatever came next, they would face it together.

As they sat together that night, their home filled with laughter and warmth, Ryan turned to David with a quiet smile. "This is everything I ever wanted," he said softly.

David leaned over, pressing a kiss to Ryan's temple. "And it's just the beginning."

Chapter 18: Building Bridges

With Devon thriving in his recovery and Hilary blossoming into a bright and curious young girl, Ryan and David found themselves reflecting on the incredible journey their family had taken. But as life seemed to settle into a harmonious rhythm, a new opportunity presented itself—one that would push them to extend their impact beyond their immediate family and community.

It began with a call from an old friend of Ryan's, Jessica, who worked at a nonprofit organization dedicated to supporting LGBTQ+ youth. The organization, Bridge the Gap, focused on providing mentorship, resources, and safe spaces for young people navigating the challenges of their identities.

"Ryan, we're launching a new program for families," Jessica explained during their conversation. "We want to help parents and guardians better support their LGBTQ+

kids. I immediately thought of you and David—you've created such a beautiful, loving family. Would you consider leading a few workshops?"

Ryan hesitated. While he and David had shared their story within their community, this felt bigger—more public. But the more he thought about it, the more he realized how essential it was. "Let me talk to David," he said. "But I think we'd love to help."

David was on board the moment Ryan brought up the idea. "If we can help even one family avoid the struggles we faced, it'll be worth it," he said. "Let's do it."

The workshops, titled Building Bridges: Strengthening Families Through Understanding, were designed to foster open communication and mutual support within families. Ryan and David shared their personal experiences, offering insights and practical tools for navigating the complexities of family dynamics and acceptance.

The first session was nerve-wracking. As Ryan stood in front of a room filled with parents, guardians, and teens, he felt a familiar flutter of anxiety. But when he looked at David, who smiled reassuringly from his place beside him, he found his confidence.

"We're not experts," Ryan began, his voice steady. "We're just two dads who love our kids and want to create a safe, supportive home for them. And we're here to share what we've learned."

The workshops quickly became a success. Families from all walks of life attended, each bringing their own unique challenges and questions. Ryan and David listened, shared advice, and created a space where people felt heard and understood.

One evening, after a particularly emotional session, a mother approached them, tears in her eyes. "My son came out to me last year," she said. "I didn't handle it well. But hearing your story… it's given me hope that I can make things right."

Ryan placed a hand on her shoulder, his voice gentle.

"It's never too late to show your love. The fact that you're here means so much."

David nodded, offering her a kind smile. "The most essential thing is that he knows you're trying. That means everything."

As they continued their work with Bridge the Gap, Ryan and David found themselves inspired by the resilience and courage of the families they met. The experience deepened their own relationship, reminding them of the strength they had found in each other and the love that had carried them through their own challenges.
One evening, after putting Hilary to bed, they sat together on the couch, reflecting on the journey they had taken.
"Do you ever think about where we started?" Ryan asked, his voice soft. "The reunion, the move to LA, everything we've been through?"

David smiled, leaning back against the cushions. "All the time. And I wouldn't change a thing."

Ryan nodded, his gaze thoughtful. "It feels like… everything we've been through led us to this. To helping others."

David reached for Ryan's hand, his touch warm and steady. "And we'll keep doing it. Together."

Their work with Bridge the Gap grew over time. They began collaborating on larger projects, from organizing community events to developing online resources that reached families across the country. Their story became a source of hope and inspiration, reminding others that love and understanding could overcome even the toughest challenges.

Through it all, Ryan and David remained grounded by their family. Hilary and Devon continued to thrive, their bond with each other and their parents growing stronger with every passing day. Their home was filled with laughter, creativity, and a sense of safety that Ryan and David had worked so hard to cultivate.

One evening, as they prepared for another workshop, Devon walked into the living room, holding one of his paintings. It was a vibrant depiction of a bridge stretching across a river, its arches illuminated by a golden sunset.

"I made this for you," he said, handing it to Ryan and David. "For everything you've done—for me, for Hilary, and for everyone you've helped. You're building bridges, just like this one."

Ryan's eyes filled with tears as he looked at the painting, the symbolism hitting him deeply. "Devon… this is beautiful. Thank you."

David smiled, wrapping an arm around Devon's shoulders. "We're so proud of you. And we couldn't have done any of this without you."
The painting found a place of honor in their shop, a daily reminder of the impact they were making as a family. It symbolized not just the bridges they had built for others, but the ones they had crossed together—the challenges

they had faced, the love that had sustained them, and the future they were creating.

As they stood together one evening, looking at the painting, Ryan turned to David with a soothing smile. "We've come so far."

David nodded, his heart full. "And the best part? We're just getting started."

Chapter 19: Celebrating Milestones

Life for Ryan and David had become a tapestry of love, community, and purpose. Each day brought its own unique challenges and joys, but it was the milestones—both big and small—that reminded them of how far they had come as individuals, as a couple, and as a family.

The first milestone was Hilary's tenth birthday, a day that felt like a culmination of everything they had dreamed of when they first decided to start a family. David spent hours decorating the backyard, stringing up lights and arranging balloons in Hilary's favorite colors, pink and gold. Ryan worked tirelessly in the kitchen, preparing Hilary's favorite dishes and baking a cake shaped like a butterfly—an homage to her love of nature.

When Hilary ran into the backyard that afternoon, her eyes widened in delight. "This is amazing!" she exclaimed, throwing her arms around Ryan and David. "Thank you!"

"You deserve it, sweetheart," David said, kissing the top of her head. "You're the best thing that's ever happened to us."

The party was a joyful affair, filled with laughter, games, and the warmth of friends and family. Devon had painted a mural on one of the garden walls as a surprise for his sister—a whimsical scene of butterflies and flowers that left Hilary speechless.

"This is the best birthday ever," Hilary said as she blew out the candles on her cake. "I love you all so much."

Ryan and David exchanged a glance, their hearts full. "We love you too," Ryan said, his voice steady with emotion. "More than you'll ever know."

Another significant milestone came when Timeless Connections celebrated its fifth anniversary. The shop had grown into a beloved community hub, attracting customers from all over the city and beyond. To mark the occasion, Ryan and David hosted an open house, inviting customers, friends, and local artists to celebrate with them.

The event was a resounding success. The shop buzzed with energy as people shared stories about the items they had purchased and the memories they had created. A local band performed in the corner, filling the space with lively music, and Devon's artwork was featured in a special exhibit that drew widespread praise.

"You've built something truly special here," a customer told Ryan as she admired the collection of antique jewelry on display. "This place isn't just a shop—it's a place where people connect."
Ryan smiled, his gaze drifting to David, who was chatting animatedly with a group of guests. "That's what we always wanted it to be," he said. "A place for connection."

The anniversary also brought an unexpected surprise. A local magazine reached out to feature Timeless Connections in an article about family-run businesses in

Los Angeles. The piece highlighted Ryan and David's journey, their commitment to preserving history, and the ways their shop had become a beacon of community.

When the article was published, Ryan and David were inundated with messages of support and congratulations. "You're an inspiration," one email read. "Your story reminds us that love and passion can create something truly beautiful."

The most emotional milestone, however, was Devon's graduation from art school. After years of hard work and dedication, he had earned his degree in art therapy—a path he had chosen not only to pursue his passion but also to help others.

The ceremony was held in a sunlit courtyard, and Ryan and David beamed with pride as Devon walked across the stage to receive his diploma. "That's our boy," David whispered, his voice thick with emotion.

After the ceremony, they celebrated with a family dinner

at Devon's favorite restaurant. As they toasted to his achievement, Devon looked at Ryan and David, his eyes shining with gratitude.

"I wouldn't be here without you," he said simply. "You believed in me when I didn't believe in myself. Thank you for everything."

Ryan reached for Devon's hand, his voice steady but filled with emotion. "We're so proud of you. And we can't wait to see what you do next."

The milestones continued to come, each one a reminder of the love and determination that had brought them to this point. Whether it was Hilary winning a science fair, Devon hosting his first art exhibit, or Ryan and David celebrating another wedding anniversary, each moment was a testament to the life they had built together.
As they sat together one evening, reflecting on their journey, Ryan turned to David with a loving smile. "Do you ever stop and think about how far we've come?"

David nodded, his hand resting on Ryan's. "Every day.
And I can't wait to see where we go from here."

Ryan smiled, his heart full. "Me too."

Chapter 20: Legacy of Love

As the years unfolded, Ryan and David began to think about the legacy they were creating—not just for their children, but for the countless lives they had touched through their work, their family, and their unwavering commitment to love and connection.

One evening, as they sat on their porch watching the sunset, Ryan turned to David with a thoughtful expression. "Do you ever wonder what people will remember about us? What we'll leave behind?"

David smiled, his gaze fixed on the horizon. "I think about it sometimes. But I don't need us to be remembered for anything grand. If people look back and see that we loved deeply, that we made a difference— even in small ways—that's enough for me."

Ryan nodded, his heart full. "I want our kids to carry that with them. To know that love is the most essential thing we ever did."

Their desire to leave a lasting impact led them to expand their work with Bridge the Gap. Together, they developed a mentorship program aimed at supporting LGBTQ+ youth transitioning out of foster care—a group that often faced significant challenges in finding stability and support.

The program, called Homebound, paired youth with mentors who could offer guidance, resources, and a sense of belonging. Ryan and David poured their hearts into the initiative, using their own experiences to shape its mission.

"This isn't just about giving kids a place to stay," Ryan explained during a meeting with potential donors. "It's about giving them a family—a community that believes in them and helps them believe in themselves."

The program quickly gained traction, attracting volunteers, funding, and recognition from local organizations. Ryan and David's home became a gathering place for the youth they mentored, filled with laughter, shared meals, and the kind of warmth that only love could provide.

Meanwhile, Hilary and Devon continued to thrive, each carving out their own paths while carrying the values their fathers had instilled in them. Hilary, now a teenager, had developed a passion for environmental science and spent her weekends volunteering at a local wildlife conservation center.

"I want to make the world a better place," she explained one afternoon as she showed Ryan and David her latest school project—a plan to reduce plastic waste in her community. "Just like you guys do."

Ryan beamed with pride. "You already are, Hilary." Devon, now a practicing art therapist, had become a beacon of hope for his clients. He often shared his own story of struggle and resilience, using his art to help others find healing and self-expression.

"You've built something incredible," Ryan told Devon during a visit to his studio. "And you've done it with so much heart."

Devon smiled, his gratitude evident. "I learned from the best."

As Ryan and David approached their fifteenth wedding anniversary, they decided to celebrate not with a lavish party, but with a relaxing evening surrounded by the people they loved most. Devon and Hilary planned a surprise dinner for them, transforming the backyard into a magical space filled with twinkling lights, music, and memories.

During the meal, Devon stood to give a toast. "To the two people who showed me what love really means," he said, his voice steady but emotional. "You've taught us that family isn't about where you come from—it's about the people who stand by you, who love you, no matter what. Thank you for everything."

Ryan and David exchanged a glance, their hearts full. "We couldn't have done any of this without all of you," Ryan said, his voice trembling with emotion. "You're our world."

As the evening drew to a close, Ryan and David sat together beneath the stars, their hands intertwined. The sounds of laughter and music drifted from the house, a reminder of the life they had built together.

"This is our legacy," Ryan said softly. "Not just the shop, or the programs, or the work we've done. It's this—our family, our love."
David nodded, his eyes shining. "And it's a legacy that will last."

Their story wasn't about perfection or grand achievements. It was about love—messy, beautiful, transformative love that had carried them through every challenge and every triumph. And as they looked toward the future, they knew that whatever came next, they would face it together, with the same courage and devotion that had brought them this far.

"Here's to us," Ryan said, raising an imaginary glass.

David grinned, leaning in to kiss him. "To us."

Chapter 21: Anchoring Each Other

Life moved forward for Ryan, David, Hilary, and Devon with a rhythm that reflected the strength of their family bond. But as they celebrated their milestones and embraced their achievements, they also learned that even the most grounded relationships require continuous care and attention.

It began with small things—missed conversations, the occasional argument over schedules, and the subtle strain of balancing their responsibilities. Between managing Timeless Connections, leading workshops for Bridge the Gap, and supporting their children, Ryan and David found themselves running on fumes.

One evening, as they sat side by side on the couch, the weight of their exhaustion finally caught up with them.

"We barely talk anymore," Ryan said softly, his voice tinged with frustration. "Not about anything that matters."

David sighed, running a hand through his hair. "I know. I feel it too. It's like… we're so busy taking care of everything else that we've forgotten to take care of us." Ryan looked at him, the vulnerability in his expression mirrored by David's. "I don't want to lose what we have."

David reached for Ryan's hand, his grip firm and reassuring. "We won't. But we need to make time—for us."

The realization marked the beginning of a new chapter in their relationship. Ryan and David made a conscious effort to prioritize their connection, carving out time for date nights, peaceful walks, and moments of reflection. They also decided to attend couples therapy—not because they were struggling, but because they wanted to strengthen their foundation.

"Therapy isn't just for when things are falling apart,"

their therapist, Dr. Morales, explained during their first session. "It's also a tool for growth. For learning how to show up for each other in new and deeper ways."

Over the weeks that followed, Ryan and David explored topics they hadn't discussed in years—how their past experiences shaped their relationship, how they communicated their needs, and how they could better support one another in the future.

"You've always been my anchor," Ryan told David during one session. "But I think sometimes I forget that you need anchoring too."

David smiled, his eyes soft. "We anchor each other. That's how it's always been."
Their renewed commitment to each other brought a sense of peace and joy that rippled through every part of their lives. They rediscovered the little things that had brought them together in the first place—shared laughter, tender moments of connection, and the unshakable belief that they were stronger together.

On one of their date nights, as they sat at their favorite rooftop restaurant overlooking the city, Ryan raised his glass with a smile. "To us," he said simply.

David clinked his glass against Ryan's, his heart full. "To us."

Chapter 22: A New Beginning for Hilary

As Hilary approached her teenage years, her curiosity and determination grew stronger. She had always been a bright and adventurous child, but now, she was beginning to think more deeply about her passions and what she wanted to do with her life.

One day, while flipping through a book about wildlife conservation, she turned to Ryan with a thoughtful expression. "Do you think I could be a scientist someday?"

Ryan smiled, setting down the cup of tea he'd been drinking. "I think you can be anything you want to be. What kind of scientist are you thinking about?"

Hilary's eyes lit up. "I want to help animals—protect them and their habitats. Like the people who save turtles and stop forests from being cut down."

David, who had been listening from across the room, walked over and placed a hand on her shoulder. "That's an amazing goal, Hilary. And knowing you, you'll make it happen."

Hilary grinned, her confidence bolstered by her fathers' unwavering support.

Her newfound passion led to hours spent researching conservation efforts and volunteering at the local wildlife center. She became a regular at their Saturday programs, learning everything from caring for injured birds to raising awareness about endangered species.

One weekend, she excitedly told Ryan and David about a turtle rescue operation she had participated in. "We helped release baby turtles into the ocean!" she exclaimed, her eyes sparkling. "It felt so good to see them swim away, knowing they have a chance."

Ryan and David exchanged a proud glance. "You're making a difference, Hilary," Ryan said, pulling her into a hug. "And we couldn't be prouder."

Her passion for conservation soon spilled into her schoolwork. For a science fair project, she designed a plan to reduce plastic waste in her school cafeteria. With Devon's help, she created a presentation complete with colorful visuals and statistics.

When she won first place, her family celebrated with a special dinner. "You're already changing the world," David told her as they raised their glasses. "And you're just getting started."

Hilary's journey reminded Ryan and David of the importance of nurturing their children's dreams, no matter how big or small. Watching her grow into a confident, compassionate young woman filled them with hope for the future.

"She's going to do incredible things," Ryan said one evening as they watched Hilary writing in her journal at the kitchen table.

David nodded, his heart full. "And we'll be right there cheering her on."

Chapter 23: Devon's First Step

Devon's art therapy career was flourishing, but he found himself grappling with a question that had lingered in the back of his mind for years: Could he open his own practice? The idea excited him, but it also terrified him. Starting a business felt daunting, and he worried about whether he was ready to take such a big leap.

One evening, as he joined Ryan and David for dinner, he decided to bring it up. "I've been thinking about starting my own art therapy studio," he said hesitantly. "But... I don't know if I can do it."

Ryan set down his fork, his expression thoughtful. "What makes you think you can't?"

Devon shrugged, staring at his plate. "It just feels... big. Like there's so much that could go wrong."

David reached across the table, his hand resting on

Devon's. "Starting a business is big," he said gently. "But that doesn't mean you can't do it. You're talented, passionate, and driven—and we're here to help."

With his fathers' encouragement, Devon began exploring the logistics of opening his own studio. Ryan shared tips from running Timeless Connections, while David helped him brainstorm ways to make his practice unique.

After months of planning, Devon found a small but charming space in a serene part of the city. With his family's help, he transformed it into a welcoming studio filled with art supplies, soothing colors, and inspirational quotes on the walls.

He named it Canvas of Hope.

The grand opening was a celebration of Devon's hard work and determination. Friends, family, and colleagues gathered to show their support, and Devon felt a surge of gratitude as he looked around the room.

"I couldn't have done this without all of you," he said during a toast. "Thank you for believing in me."

Ryan and David beamed with pride. "You've always had it in you," Ryan said, raising his glass. "We just helped you see it."

Devon's studio quickly became a safe space for his clients, many of whom were teenagers and young adults navigating their own challenges. Watching them find healing and self-expression through art reaffirmed Devon's belief in his work.

As he shared stories about his clients during family dinners, Ryan and David couldn't help but marvel at how far he had come.

"You're changing lives, Devon," David said one evening, his voice filled with emotion. "And we couldn't be prouder."

Chapter 24: The Strength of Friendship

As Ryan and David's lives evolved, so did their relationships with their close friends, particularly Alex and Miguel. The two couples had been inseparable since Ryan and David first moved to Los Angeles, and their bond only grew stronger with time. But like any relationship, it required care and understanding.

One evening, Alex invited Ryan and David over for dinner, his voice on the phone unusually strained. "It's been a while since we've all caught up," he said. "Miguel and I could really use some company."

When they arrived, the tension in the air was palpable. Miguel greeted them with a forced smile, and Alex seemed distracted as he set the table. Over the course of the meal, the cracks in their relationship began to show—snippy comments, long silences, and an undercurrent of frustration that neither could fully hide.

After dinner, as the four of them sat in the living room, Alex finally broke down. "We've been struggling," he admitted, his voice trembling. "We've just been so busy—Miguel with his work, me with mine. It feels like we're drifting apart."

Ryan and David exchanged a glance, their hearts aching for their friends. They understood all too well the challenges of balancing work, family, and a relationship.

"Have you talked about it?" Ryan asked gently. Miguel sighed, running a hand through his hair. "We've tried. But it's like… we don't know how anymore."

Over the next few weeks, Ryan and David made it their mission to support Alex and Miguel. They encouraged them to attend couples therapy, shared their own experiences, and spent time with them in ways that reminded them of the joy and love that had always defined their relationship.

One evening, as they sat around a bonfire at the beach,

Alex turned to Ryan and David with a small smile. "Thank you," he said simply. "For not giving up on us."

Miguel nodded, his expression softer than it had been in months. "We're still a work in progress, but… we're starting to find our way back to each other."

Ryan reached for David's hand, his heart swelling with pride for their friends. "That's all that matters," he said. "Love is worth fighting for."

Chapter 25: Devon's First Challenge

While Canvas of Hope was thriving, Devon soon faced his first major challenge as a business owner. A client's parent filed a complaint, claiming that Devon's methods were "unconventional" and questioning whether art therapy was a legitimate form of treatment.

The complaint shook Devon's confidence. "What if they're right?" he said one evening as he sat with Ryan and David at the kitchen table. "What if I'm not cut out for this?"

Ryan placed a comforting hand on his shoulder. "Devon, you've worked so hard to get here. One complaint doesn't define your abilities or the impact you've made."

David nodded. "Remember why you started this—to help people heal. And you've already done that for so many."

With their encouragement, Devon decided to address the situation head-on. He met with the parent, listened to their concerns, and explained the principles behind art therapy and its proven benefits. To his relief, the conversation ended on a positive note, with the parent expressing a better understanding of his methods.

"That took courage," Ryan told Devon later that evening. "And it shows how much you care about your work."

Devon smiled, his confidence slowly returning. "I guess I just needed to be reminded of why I started."

Chapter 26: Hilary's Big Idea

Hilary's passion for conservation continued to grow, and with it, her desire to make a larger impact. Inspired by a documentary about grassroots environmental movements, she decided to start a school club focused on sustainability.

"I want to call it 'Eco Warriors,'" she announced during dinner one evening. "We'll organize cleanups, plant trees, and teach people how to reduce waste."

Ryan and David exchanged a proud glance. "That's an incredible idea," David said. "How can we help?"

Over the next few weeks, the family worked together to bring Hilary's vision to life. They helped her design flyers, plan activities, and secure permission from her school principal. The club's first event—a community cleanup at a local park—was a resounding success, drawing dozens of participants and earning praise from the local newspaper.

"I can't believe this is really happening," Hilary said as she stood with her family at the end of the event, looking out at the bags of trash they had collected. "We're making a difference."

Ryan wrapped an arm around her shoulders, his heart swelling with pride. "You're making a difference, Hilary. And we couldn't be prouder."

Chapter 27: Ryan's Unexpected Journey

Amid the bustling life of their family, Ryan found himself craving a new challenge. Running Timeless Connections had been deeply fulfilling, but after years of pouring his heart into the shop, he began to wonder what else he could contribute to the world.

One afternoon, as he sorted through a box of vintage letters for the shop, he stumbled upon a note written in elegant cursive. It was from a man to his lover during World War II, filled with longing, hope, and an unwavering belief in their love.

Ryan read the letter aloud to David later that evening. "It's incredible how love finds a way, even in the hardest of times," he said, his voice filled with emotion.

David smiled, his hand resting on Ryan's. "You've always had a way of seeing the beauty in stories like this.

Maybe there's something more you can do with it."

The idea took root. Inspired by the countless stories he had uncovered through the shop, Ryan decided to start a blog called Love Through Time, where he would share the letters, photographs, and mementos that spoke to the enduring power of love.

The blog quickly gained traction, attracting readers from around the world who were moved by the stories Ryan curated. Comments poured in from people who related to the tales of love, loss, and resilience.

"This has become so much more than I imagined," Ryan told David one evening as they reviewed the latest responses. "It's like I'm connecting with people on a whole new level."

David smiled, his pride evident. "Because you're reminding them of something we all need—hope."

Chapter 28: A New Chapter for Alex and Miguel

While Ryan and David focused on their own journeys, their closest friends Alex and Miguel were navigating a significant change. After months of reflection and hard work, they decided to renew their vows, a gesture that symbolized their recommitment to each other and the life they had built together.

"We want you to officiate," Alex told Ryan and David over dinner one evening. "You've been there for us through everything, and it would mean the world to have you by our side."

Ryan and David were honored. "We'd be thrilled," David said, his eyes shining with emotion. "You two are such an essential part of our lives."

The vow renewal ceremony was held at the beach, a place that had always been special to both couples.

Under a canopy of twinkling lights, Alex and Miguel exchanged heartfelt promises, their love for each other as strong as ever.

Ryan and David couldn't help but feel a renewed sense of gratitude for their own relationship as they watched their friends take this meaningful step.

"Love takes work," Ryan said as they walked along the shore after the ceremony. "But it's always worth it." David nodded, his hand clasping Ryan's. "It always is."

Chapter 29: Hilary's First Challenge

Hilary's Eco Warriors club had quickly become one of the most active groups at her school, but success brought its own challenges. When the club proposed replacing single-use plastics in the cafeteria with reusable options, they faced resistance from school administrators who were concerned about costs.

"They don't see the bigger picture," Hilary said, her frustration evident as she recounted the meeting to Ryan and David. "This isn't just about money—it's about protecting the planet."

Ryan placed a reassuring hand on her shoulder. "Big changes take time, Hilary. But you've already shown that you can make a difference. Don't give up."

David nodded. "And remember, you're not alone. Your club, your family—we're all here to support you."

With her parents' encouragement, Hilary rallied her club members to gather data on the environmental and financial benefits of reusable materials. They presented their findings to the school board, earning praise for their thoroughness and passion.

When the board approved a pilot program to reduce plastic waste, Hilary's determination paid off. "We did it!" she exclaimed, running into the house with the good news. "They're actually going to try it!"

Ryan and David exchanged a proud glance. "You're proving that even small changes can lead to something big," Ryan said.

Hilary beamed. "Thanks for believing in me."

Chapter 30: Devon's Breakthrough

As Devon's art therapy practice grew, he began exploring innovative ways to help his clients express themselves. One idea stood out—a community mural project where his clients could collaborate on a large-scale piece that represented their collective journey of healing and hope.

"It's ambitious," he admitted during a family dinner. "But I think it could be really powerful."

Ryan and David immediately supported the idea. "You've always been about helping people find their voice," David said. "This is just another way to do that."

With the help of local organizations and volunteers, Devon secured a wall in a busy part of the city. Over several weeks, his clients worked together to design and paint the mural, sharing their stories and supporting one another along the way.

When the mural was unveiled, it was met with overwhelming praise. Titled Rising Together, it depicted a vibrant phoenix surrounded by interconnected hands, symbolizing resilience and unity.

Devon stood with his family at the unveiling, his heart swelling with pride. "This isn't just about me," he said. "It's about everyone who's been brave enough to tell their story."

Ryan wrapped an arm around him. "And it's about the impact you've made."

Chapter 31: Hilary's Leadership Grows

Hilary's success with the Eco Warriors club had given her a sense of purpose, but it also came with new challenges. As her peers looked to her for guidance, she realized the weight of leadership was heavier than she had anticipated.

One afternoon, as she worked on a presentation for an upcoming school-wide assembly about environmental initiatives, Ryan found her staring blankly at her laptop.

"Everything okay?" he asked, sitting down beside her.

Hilary sighed, resting her chin in her hand. "I don't know if I can do this. What if they don't take me seriously? What if they think it's dumb?"

Ryan placed a reassuring hand on her shoulder. "Hilary, you've already shown that you're capable of leading. The plastic waste program was your idea, and it's making a difference. This is just the next step."

David chimed in from the doorway. "And remember, leadership isn't about being perfect. It's about caring enough to try."

At the assembly, Hilary stood nervously on the stage as hundreds of students filed into the auditorium. But as she began to speak, her passion took over. She shared her vision for a cleaner, more sustainable future, her voice steady and filled with conviction. By the end of her presentation, the audience erupted in applause.

"That was amazing," one of her teachers told her afterward. "You've inspired so many people today."

Hilary's smile was radiant as she joined her family later that evening. "I guess I'm not so bad at this leadership thing after all."

Ryan pulled her into a hug. "Not bad? Hilary, you're a natural."

Chapter 32: Devon's New Challenge

While Hilary was thriving in her role as a young leader, Devon faced his own set of challenges at Canvas of Hope. His client base was growing, and with it came the need to expand his services. But managing the increased demand while maintaining the personal touch his clients valued was proving difficult.

"I feel like I'm stretched too thin," Devon admitted during a family dinner. "I want to help everyone, but I can't do it all on my own."

David, always the problem-solver, suggested bringing in an assistant or another therapist to share the workload. "You don't have to do this alone," he said. "Building a team doesn't mean you care less—it means you can do more."

Devon hesitated, worried about losing the intimate atmosphere he had worked so hard to create. But after some encouragement from Ryan and David, he decided to give it a try.

Hiring his first team member, a fellow art therapist named Clara, was a turning point for Devon. Together, they introduced new programs, including group therapy sessions and art workshops for families. The expanded services not only helped Devon manage his workload but also allowed Canvas of Hope to reach even more people.

One evening, after a particularly successful workshop, Devon reflected on the journey with Ryan and David. "I was so scared of losing what I'd built," he said. "But now it feels like I've gained so much more."

Ryan smiled, his pride evident. "Because you were willing to take a risk. And it paid off."

Chapter 33: A Family Reunion

While their lives in Los Angeles were full and vibrant, Ryan and David realized they had been neglecting some of their extended family back in Georgia. When Hilary asked about her grandparents during a quiet evening at home, Ryan felt a pang of guilt.

"They haven't seen Hilary or Devon in years," Ryan said to David later that evening. "Maybe it's time for a visit."

David nodded. "It's long overdue."

The trip to Georgia was filled with emotion. Ryan's mother welcomed them with open arms, her joy at seeing Hilary and Devon evident in the way she fussed over them.

"You've grown so much!" she exclaimed, pulling Hilary into a tight hug. "And Devon, look at you—all grown up and making a difference."

The visit was a reminder of where they had come from, the values instilled in them by their families, and the resilience that had carried them through life's challenges.

"I'm so proud of the life you've built," Ryan's mother told him one evening as they sat on the porch. "And I'm so glad you brought them here. They're amazing kids."

Ryan's heart swelled with gratitude. "I learned from the best."

Chapter 34: Timeless Connections Expands

Back in Los Angeles, Timeless Connections continued to thrive, but Ryan and David noticed a growing demand for more interactive experiences. Inspired by the success of community events, they decided to open a second location that focused on workshops and storytelling sessions.

"This isn't just a shop—it's a space for people to connect," David said during one of their planning meetings. "Let's make the new location a place where history comes alive."

The second location, Timeless Connections: The Experience, opened to great acclaim. Visitors could learn how to restore vintage items, participate in storytelling nights, and even bring in their own heirlooms to share with the community.

"This is exactly what we envisioned," Ryan said during

the grand opening. "A place where the past meets the present."

Chapter 35: Devon's First Public Recognition

Devon's work at Canvas of Hope caught the attention of a local nonprofit that recognized individuals making a significant impact on mental health in the community. When they nominated him for an award, Devon was both honored and nervous.

"I'm not doing this for recognition," he told Ryan and David. "But it feels… good to be seen."

On the night of the award ceremony, the entire family turned out to support him. As Devon accepted the award, his voice was steady but emotional.

"This isn't just about me," he said. "It's about every person who's ever had the courage to tell their story. And it's about the people who believed in me when I didn't believe in myself. Thank you."

Devon's recognition was a reminder of the ripple effect of their family's love and support. As they celebrated together that evening, Ryan turned to David with a loving smile. "This is what it's all about."

David nodded, his heart full. "It always has been."

Chapter 36: Hilary's First Protest

Hilary's growing awareness of environmental issues led her to take on even larger challenges. When a proposed development project threatened a local wildlife preserve, she decided to take a stand.

"I can't just sit back and let this happen," Hilary announced at dinner one evening. "They're planning to destroy habitats for so many animals."

Ryan and David exchanged a glance, impressed by her determination. "What do you want to do about it?" Ryan asked.

Hilary grinned, already brimming with ideas. "I want to organize a protest. Something that'll show how much this place means to people."

The planning took weeks. With her Eco Warriors club, Hilary coordinated volunteers, created posters, and spread the word on social media. Ryan and David helped where they could, offering advice and resources while ensuring she felt empowered to take the lead.

The day of the protest, dozens of people gathered at the preserve, holding signs and chanting slogans. Hilary stood at the front, addressing the crowd with the confidence of someone twice her age.

"This isn't just about the animals," she said, her voice strong. "It's about all of us. Protecting this land means protecting our future."

Her words resonated, and local media picked up the story. While the battle to save the preserve was far from over, Hilary's efforts sparked a wave of support and awareness.

"You're unstoppable," David told her that evening as they celebrated with pizza. "I'm so proud of you."

Hilary beamed. "I'm just getting started."

Chapter 37: Ryan's First Public Talk

Ryan's blog, Love Through Time, had grown into a significant platform, and its success brought an unexpected opportunity. A university invited him to give a lecture about the power of historical artifacts in connecting generations.

"I don't know if I can do this," Ryan admitted to David as he prepared his presentation. "I've never spoken in front of so many people."

David placed a reassuring hand on his shoulder. "You've been sharing these stories for years. This is just another way to do it. You've got this."

On the day of the lecture, Ryan stood nervously in front of a packed auditorium. But as he began to speak, his passion took over. He shared stories from the shop, letters from his blog, and the profound connections he had witnessed through the artifacts he'd preserved.

Afterward, the applause was deafening. Several students approached him with questions, eager to learn more about his work.

"You have a gift," one student said. "Thank you for sharing these stories."

Ryan left the lecture feeling a renewed sense of purpose. "Maybe I could do more of this," he told David later that evening. "It feels good to share what I've learned." David smiled, his pride evident. "I think you've found your next calling."

Chapter 38: Devon's Art Exhibit

As Devon's confidence grew, so did his ambition. He decided to curate his first solo art exhibit, showcasing pieces that reflected his journey and the stories of his clients (anonymized, of course).

The exhibit, titled Healing Through Color, was held at a local gallery and featured vibrant, emotional works that explored themes of resilience, hope, and transformation.

On opening night, the gallery was packed with supporters, including Ryan, David, Hilary, and many of Devon's clients.

"This isn't just art," one attendee remarked. "It's a testament to the human spirit."

Devon smiled, his heart swelling with pride. "That's exactly what I hoped for."

Chapter 39: A New Addition to the Family

Life for Ryan, David, Hilary, and Devon was full, but they began to feel that something—or someone—was missing. After much discussion, they decided to welcome a rescue dog into their family.

The moment they saw the scrappy, one-eyed mutt at the shelter, they knew he was the one. "He's been through a lot," the shelter worker explained. "But he's got so much love to give."

They named him Lucky, and he quickly became the heart of their household. Whether it was accompanying Ryan to the shop, playing with Hilary in the yard, or curling up beside Devon as he painted, Lucky brought a new layer of joy to their lives.

"This house feels even more like home now," Ryan said one evening as Lucky snored at his feet.
David smiled. "He's a reminder that love can heal

anything.”

Chapter 40: A Family Celebration

With so many milestones behind them, Ryan and David decided it was time to celebrate everything their family had accomplished. They hosted a backyard barbecue, inviting friends, neighbors, and colleagues to join in the festivities.

As the sun set and the garden filled with laughter and music, Ryan looked around at the people who had become part of their journey.

"This is what it's all about," he said to David. "All of us, together."

David nodded, his heart full. "We've built something amazing. And it's just the beginning."

Chapter 41: Hilary's Ambitious Project

Hilary's success with the Eco Warriors club and her protest left her eager for her next challenge. She wanted to make a broader, lasting impact, and an idea began forming during a class discussion about renewable energy.

"What if our school could use solar panels?" she asked her teacher. "It would save money and help the environment."

Her teacher was intrigued. "That's ambitious, Hilary. But if anyone can figure it out, it's you."

That evening, Hilary shared her idea with Ryan and David. "It's a big project, but I think it's worth it," she said, her excitement palpable. "We'd need funding and approval, but imagine what it could do for the school."

Ryan smiled, recognizing her determination. "You've

always dreamed big, Hilary. Let's figure out how to make this happen."

David nodded in agreement. "We'll help you create a proposal. You'll need research, cost analysis, and a plan to present to the school board."

Over the next several weeks, the family worked together on the project. Hilary researched grants and solar companies, while Ryan helped her create a presentation that outlined the environmental and financial benefits. David reached out to local organizations that might support the initiative.

The night before her presentation to the school board, Hilary was visibly nervous. "What if they say no?" she asked, pacing the living room.

Ryan knelt in front of her, his expression gentle. "Then you'll try again, or find another way. But you've worked hard, Hilary, and no matter what happens, we're so proud of you."

David smiled. "You've already inspired people just by trying. That's what real leadership is."

The presentation was a success. Hilary spoke with passion and confidence, answering questions from board members and sharing testimonials from students and teachers who supported the project.

When the school board voted to approve the initial phase, the room erupted in applause. Hilary's classmates and teachers surrounded her, offering congratulations.

At home that evening, Hilary hugged Ryan and David tightly. "We did it," she said, her voice full of awe.

Ryan beamed. "No, you did it. We just helped."

David nodded. "And this is just the beginning."

Chapter 42: Devon's Mentorship Role

As Canvas of Hope continued to thrive, Devon found himself in a new role: mentor. Several young therapists reached out to him for advice, inspired by his work and his unique approach to art therapy.

One young woman, Sofia, stood out. She had recently graduated from art school and wanted to follow in Devon's footsteps. "I don't know where to start," she admitted during their first meeting. "I want to help people, but it feels overwhelming."

Devon saw himself in Sofia—eager but unsure. "It's okay to feel that way," he said. "The essential thing is to remember why you're doing this. The rest will fall into place."

Devon began mentoring Sofia, inviting her to observe sessions, sharing resources, and encouraging her to develop her own style. Over time, Sofia grew more confident, and Devon realized how much he enjoyed helping others find their path.

"You've been incredible at this," Ryan told Devon one evening after Sofia stopped by to thank him. "You're not just helping your clients—you're shaping the future of this field."

Devon smiled, his pride evident. "It feels good to give back. I wouldn't be here without the people who believed in me."

Chapter 43: Ryan's Growing Platform

Ryan's blog, Love Through Time, continued to grow, and its popularity opened doors he hadn't anticipated. One day, he received an invitation to write a book—a collection of letters, artifacts, and stories from the shop that celebrated the enduring power of love.

"I don't know if I can do this," Ryan said, showing the email to David. "A book feels… huge."

David grinned. "You've been writing these stories for years. You've got this, Ryan."

The process was daunting but rewarding. Ryan spent months curating letters, interviewing customers, and weaving their stories into a narrative that captured the essence of Timeless Connections. David and Devon helped with editing, while Hilary offered her insights on the visual design.

When the book, Stories That Bind Us, was published, it became an instant success. Readers from all over the world praised its heartwarming and poignant tales.

At a book signing event, a woman approached Ryan with tears in her eyes. "Your book reminded me of my grandparents' love story," she said. "Thank you for helping me reconnect with them."

Ryan's heart swelled. "That means everything to me. Thank you for sharing that."

Chapter 44: Lucky's Journey

Lucky, the rescue dog who had become a beloved member of the family, had his own story to tell. Despite his scrappy appearance and rough beginnings, Lucky had a resilience that inspired everyone around him.

One day, Hilary suggested sharing Lucky's story at a community event. "People need to see how much love and joy a rescue dog can bring," she said.

The event, hosted by a local animal shelter, featured Lucky as the star of the show. David told his story, from his rescue to his new life with their family, and encouraged others to consider adopting pets in need.

"Lucky may have started out with one eye and a rough past," David said, his voice warm. "But he's shown us that love and kindness can transform anything." Lucky's story touched countless hearts. The shelter reported an increase in adoptions after the event, and

Lucky became something of a local celebrity.

At home, Ryan patted Lucky's head, smiling as he watched him curl up at Hilary's feet. "You're proof that second chances are worth it," he said softly. "For all of us."

Chapter 45: A Wedding to Remember

The family received joyful news when one of their closest friends, Alex, proposed to Miguel. After years of love and growth, the couple decided to renew their vows with a formal wedding ceremony that celebrated their journey.

They asked Ryan and David to be their best men, a request that filled them with pride. "You've been with us through everything," Alex said. "We couldn't imagine this day without you."

The wedding, held at a beautiful garden venue, was a celebration of love, resilience, and community. Ryan and David gave heartfelt speeches, sharing memories and expressing their admiration for Alex and Miguel.

"To love through all of life's challenges—that's what makes a relationship strong," Ryan said. "And you two are the perfect example of that."

David added with a smile, "You've shown us all what it means to choose love every single day."

The ceremony reminded Ryan and David of their own journey, reigniting their gratitude for the life they had built together. As they danced under the stars, surrounded by friends and family, Ryan leaned into David and whispered, "This feels like the start of something new."

David smiled, his heart full. "It always does—with you."

Chapter 46: Hilary's New Adventure

Hilary's environmental advocacy continued to grow, and her passion for sustainability led her to a new opportunity: a spot in a prestigious summer camp focused on climate science and leadership. Held in a lush national park, the program would allow Hilary to work with experts, participate in hands-on projects, and collaborate with other young environmentalists.

When she received her acceptance letter, she could barely contain her excitement. "I got in!" she shouted, waving the letter in the air as she ran into the living room.

Ryan pulled her into a hug. "That's amazing, Hilary! You're going to learn so much."

David smiled, his pride evident. "And you'll come back with even more ways to make a difference."

The weeks leading up to the camp were a flurry of preparation. Hilary packed and repacked her bags, researched the program's projects, and practiced her presentation skills. On the morning of her departure, the entire family piled into the car to see her off.

As they hugged goodbye, Hilary turned to Ryan and David with a determined smile. "I'm going to make you proud."

David rested a hand on her shoulder. "You already have."

At the camp, Hilary thrived. She participated in field studies, learned about renewable energy solutions, and even led her team in designing a project to reduce deforestation in urban areas. Her letters and video calls home were filled with excitement as she shared her experiences.

On the final day of camp, parents were invited to attend a showcase of the participants' projects. Hilary stood on stage, presenting her team's work with confidence and passion. As she spoke, Ryan and David exchanged a proud glance, their hearts swelling with love for their daughter.

When the presentation ended, they rushed to hug her. "You were incredible," Ryan said. "The world needs people like you."

Hilary beamed. "And I'm just getting started."

Chapter 47: Devon's Crossroads

Devon's work at Canvas of Hope was flourishing, but he began to feel a pull toward something more. While he loved his clients and the creative nature of art therapy, he started wondering if he could make an even larger impact by teaching.

"I've been thinking about becoming a professor," Devon admitted one evening during a family dinner. "Sharing what I've learned with future therapists."

Ryan and David listened intently, sensing the weight of his decision. "That's a big step," Ryan said. "But it sounds like something you're passionate about."

David nodded. "You've always been great at mentoring. Teaching would let you inspire even more people."

Devon began exploring the possibility, speaking with professors he admired and researching academic programs. After weeks of reflection, he decided to apply for a master's degree in counseling and art therapy—a step that would allow him to transition into academia while continuing his practice.

The acceptance letter arrived one sunny afternoon, and Devon burst into the shop where Ryan was working, waving the envelope. "I got in!" he exclaimed, his eyes bright with excitement.

Ryan hugged him tightly. "You're going to be amazing, Devon. You've found your path."

David joined them later that evening to celebrate. "You've always had a way of connecting with people," he said. "Now you'll get to help the next generation same."

Chapter 48: A Test for Ryan and David

While their children were pursuing new opportunities, Ryan and David faced their own challenge: an unexpected financial strain. Between the expansion of Timeless Connections and the costs of supporting Hilary and Devon's ambitions, their budget was tighter than ever.

"We're stretched thin," Ryan said one evening as they reviewed their expenses. "But I don't want to hold the kids back."

David nodded, his brow furrowed. "We'll figure it out. We've faced tougher times before."

The couple decided to make temporary adjustments, cutting back on personal luxuries and finding creative ways to save. Ryan began offering virtual workshops through the shop, while David took on additional consulting work for community programs.

The period of financial strain tested their patience and resilience, but it also reminded them of their shared strength. "We've always been a team," David said one evening as they sat together on the couch. "And we'll get through this together."

Ryan smiled, leaning against him. "We always do."

Their efforts paid off, and within a few months, their finances stabilized. The experience brought them closer, reinforcing their commitment to supporting their family and each other.

"You've always been my rock," Ryan told David one evening as they reflected on their journey. "And I'm so grateful for you."

David kissed his forehead. "We're in this together. Always."

Chapter 49: Hilary's Homecoming

When Hilary returned from her summer camp, she was bursting with new ideas and energy. "We learned so much," she said during a family dinner. "And I can't wait to start making changes at school and in the community."

She proposed hosting a sustainability fair, inviting local organizations, businesses, and students to showcase eco-friendly solutions. Ryan and David immediately supported the idea, helping her with logistics and connecting her with potential partners.

The fair was a huge success, drawing hundreds of attendees and inspiring new initiatives across the city. Hilary's leadership and passion shone brightly, earning her praise from teachers, peers, and even local media.

"You've created something amazing," Ryan said as they packed up after the event. "And you've shown people what's possible."

Hilary smiled, her heart full. "I couldn't have done it without you."

Chapter 50: A Surprise for Ryan

As Ryan approached his 45th birthday, David and the kids decided to plan a surprise celebration that would honor his journey and the impact he had made on their lives. They reached out to friends, family, and even customers from Timeless Connections to create a video montage of heartfelt messages.

On the day of the party, Ryan was stunned to find their backyard transformed into a celebration of his life. The video played on a projector, featuring stories and messages of gratitude that brought tears to his eyes.

"You've touched so many lives," David said, wrapping an arm around him. "And we're so lucky to have you."

Ryan looked around at the people he loved, his heart overflowing. "This is the best gift I could ever ask for. Thank you."

Chapter 51: Hilary's Community Recognition

Hilary's work with the Eco Warriors and her sustainability initiatives did not go unnoticed. A local environmental organization nominated her for the Young Changemaker Award, an honor given to students who demonstrate exceptional leadership in environmental advocacy.

When the nomination letter arrived, Hilary couldn't believe her eyes. "They picked me?" she said, holding the letter as if it might disappear.

Ryan smiled, pulling her into a hug. "Of course they did. You've worked so hard for this."

David nodded. "And it's well deserved."

The award ceremony was held in a grand theater downtown, filled with activists, community leaders, and supporters. Hilary's name was called, and she walked onto the stage, her heart pounding but her smile steady.

In her acceptance speech, she spoke about the power of youth to drive change. "We may be young, but our voices matter. The future is ours to shape, and we have the responsibility to protect it."

Ryan and David sat in the audience, tears in their eyes as they watched their daughter inspire an entire room.

"You've shown the world what we've always known," David said later that evening. "You're unstoppable."

Hilary grinned. "I've got you to thank for that."

Chapter 52: Devon's First Class

As Devon began his master's program, he was given the opportunity to teach an introductory course on art therapy as a teaching assistant. While he was excited about the chance, he couldn't help but feel nervous.

"What if I'm not good at this?" he asked Ryan one evening, pacing the living room.

Ryan placed a hand on his shoulder. "Devon, you've been teaching through your practice for years. This is just a new setting. You've got this."

On the first day of class, Devon walked into the lecture hall, his palms sweaty but his resolve strong. He started with an icebreaker, encouraging students to share why they were interested in art therapy. By the end of the session, the energy in the room was palpable, and Devon felt a sense of accomplishment he hadn't expected.

One of his students approached him afterward. "You're really inspiring," she said. "I wasn't sure if this was the right path for me, but now I think it is."

Devon smiled, his confidence growing. "Thank you. That means a lot."

Teaching quickly became a passion for Devon, and he began to see it as more than just a part of his program— it was a calling.

"You've found your place," Ryan told him after his first semester. "And we couldn't be prouder."

Chapter 53: David's New Initiative

David, inspired by the growth of his family and the success of Bridge the Gap, decided to start his own community program aimed at supporting LGBTQ+ families. The program, called Prideful Connections, would offer resources, workshops, and events to help families navigate their journeys with love and understanding.

"I want to create a space where families can learn, grow, and support each other," David explained to Ryan one evening. "Like we've always tried to do."

Ryan smiled, his pride evident. "You've always had a way of bringing people together. This is going to change lives."

The first Prideful Connections event was held at a local community center, featuring panel discussions, breakout sessions, and activities for kids. Families from all over the city attended, sharing stories and building connections that would last long after the event ended.

One parent approached David afterward, tears in her eyes. "You've given me hope," she said. "Thank you for creating this space."
David's heart swelled. "You're not alone. And we'll keep building this together."

Chapter 54: A Family Trip to Remember

After years of hard work and growth, Ryan and David decided it was time for a family vacation—a chance to reconnect and create new memories. They chose Alaska, a place Ryan had always dreamed of visiting but had never been.

"This is going to be amazing," Hilary said as they boarded the plane. "I've never seen snow like this before!"

Devon grinned. "Just wait until you see the glaciers."

The trip was filled with adventure. They went dog sledding, hiked through breathtaking landscapes, and marveled at the northern lights. One evening, as they sat around a campfire, Ryan looked at his family, the glow of the flames illuminating their faces.

"This is everything," he said softly. "Being here with all of you."

David reached for his hand. "We've come so far. And there's so much more ahead."

The trip was a reminder of the love that had carried them through every challenge and triumph. As they flew back home, their hearts were full, and their bond stronger than ever.

Chapter 55: A Community Award for Ryan and David

Ryan and David's work with Timeless Connections, Bridge the Gap, and Prideful Connections earned them recognition from the city. They were nominated for the Heart of the Community Award, given to individuals who had made a lasting impact on Los Angeles.

When they received the letter, Ryan was stunned. "This is… unexpected," he said, handing the letter to David.

David smiled, his eyes shining. "It's deserved. You've poured your heart into everything you've done."

At the award ceremony, they stood on stage together, surrounded by friends, family, and community members. In his acceptance speech, Ryan spoke about the journey that had brought them to this moment.

"We didn't set out to change the world," he said. "We

just wanted to create spaces where people could connect, heal, and grow. This award is a reflection of all the love and support we've received along the way."

David added, "And it's a reminder that when we come together as a community, we can achieve anything."

The audience erupted in applause, and as Ryan and David left the stage, they knew they had created something truly special.

Chapter 56: A Home Full of History

As life moved forward, Ryan and David's home became a living testament to the journey they had shared. Every room held memories, from Devon's first art project displayed in the hallway to Hilary's school trophies lining the living room shelves.

One rainy afternoon, Ryan decided to organize a box of old letters and photographs he had collected over the years from Timeless Connections. As he sifted through the items, he found a black-and-white photograph of a young couple standing in front of a 1920s farmhouse.

David walked into the room and noticed Ryan's contemplative expression. "What's that?" he asked, sitting beside him.

Ryan handed him the photo. "Just something that reminds me of us. It's a reminder of all the love that's passed through our lives, even the love of people we've never met."

David smiled. "Maybe it's time to preserve our story too."

Inspired by the idea, Ryan and David began creating a family scrapbook. It became a collaborative project, with Hilary and Devon contributing drawings, photos, and written reflections. Even Lucky had his paw print added to a page.

"This isn't just about us," Hilary said one evening as she worked on a page dedicated to her Eco Warriors club. "It's about everything we've been a part of."

Ryan nodded, his heart full. "And everything we'll continue to build."

The scrapbook became a cherished family tradition, updated regularly with new milestones and memories. It was a tangible reminder of their love, resilience, and the incredible life they had created together.

Chapter 57: Devon's Graduation

Years of hard work culminated in Devon's graduation from his master's program, a moment that marked not only his academic achievements but also the growth he had experienced as a person.

The ceremony was held in a grand auditorium, filled with students and their families. Ryan and David sat in the audience, holding hands as they waited for Devon's name to be called.

When it finally was, Devon walked across the stage with a confident stride, his cap and gown swaying with each step. As he accepted his diploma, he glanced into the audience and found his family, their cheers louder than anyone else's.

After the ceremony, they gathered for a celebratory dinner. Devon raised his glass, his voice steady but emotional. "I couldn't have done this without all of you.

You believed in me when I didn't believe in myself. Thank you for being my foundation."

Ryan smiled, his eyes glistening. "We're so proud of you, Devon. You've always had the strength to do this— you just needed to see it."

David nodded, his heart full. "And this is just the beginning."

Chapter 58: Hilary's High School Graduation

Hilary's high school graduation was another emotional milestone for the family. She had grown into a confident, compassionate young woman, ready to take on the world.

On the morning of the ceremony, Hilary stood in front of the mirror, adjusting her cap and gown. "It feels surreal," she said. "Like I was just starting high school yesterday."

Ryan smiled, placing a hand on her shoulder. "You've accomplished so much, Hilary. And you've done it all with grace and determination."

David added, "We couldn't be prouder of the person you've become."

During the ceremony, Hilary delivered the valedictorian

speech, her words resonating with everyone in the crowd. "The future is ours to create," she said. "Let's build it with kindness, courage, and a commitment to making the world a better place."

Afterward, the family celebrated with a backyard party, complete with decorations, food, and a slideshow of Hilary's achievements. As they sat together under the stars, Hilary turned to Ryan and David with a grateful smile.

"Thank you," she said softly. "For always believing in me."

Ryan hugged her tightly. "We always will."

Chapter 59: A New Chapter for Ryan and David

With Hilary heading off to college and Devon pursuing his teaching career, Ryan and David found themselves entering a new phase of life. Their home, once filled with the constant hum of activity, now felt quieter. But instead of feeling bittersweet, they saw it as an opportunity to focus on each other.

One evening, as they sat on the porch watching the sunset, Ryan turned to David with a thoughtful expression. "We've spent so much time building this life for our family. Maybe it's time we did something for us."

David raised an eyebrow. "What are you thinking?"

"A trip," Ryan said, his eyes lighting up. "Somewhere we've always wanted to go."

David smiled, his mind racing with possibilities. "Italy?"

Ryan grinned. "Italy."

The trip became a dream come true. They wandered through the cobblestone streets of Florence, marveled at the ruins of Rome, and shared tranquil moments on the canals of Venice. It was a time to reconnect, reflect, and celebrate the love that had carried them through every chapter of their lives.

"This is what it's all about," Ryan said one evening as they sat on a balcony overlooking the Tuscan countryside. "Being with you."

David reached for his hand. "And it always will be."

Chapter 60: Full Circle

As the years passed, Ryan and David's family continued to grow—not just through their children's achievements but through the relationships they had built with their community. Timeless Connections, Bridge the Gap, and Prideful Connections all thrived, leaving a lasting legacy of love and connection.

One afternoon, Ryan and David stood in the shop, now bustling with customers of all ages. A young couple approached them, holding hands and smiling nervously.

"Your shop has been such an inspiration to us," the woman said. "It reminds us of what's really essential— love and history."

Ryan's heart swelled. "That's all we've ever wanted to share."

As the couple walked away, David turned to Ryan with a

warm smile. "Do you realize how many lives we've touched?"

Ryan nodded, his eyes glistening. "It's humbling. But it's also a reminder of how much love we've been given."

That evening, the family gathered for dinner, the house filled with laughter and warmth. As they sat around the table, Ryan raised his glass.

"To love," he said simply. "To the love that's carried us through everything."

David clinked his glass against Ryan's. "And to the love that will carry us through everything to come."

As the table erupted in cheers, Ryan and David exchanged a glance, knowing that their journey—filled with challenges, triumphs, and an unshakable bond— was a testament to the enduring power of love.

What happens next will change everything…

About the Author

Robert Anthony Newsome-White is a writer, crisis counselor, clinical psychology student, and truck driver whose life is a testament to resilience and determination. Raised in a loving but challenging environment, Robert overcame personal hardships to pursue a career helping others find hope and healing.

As a proud member of the LGBTQ+ community, Robert draws on his own experiences of growth, love, and acceptance, sharing stories that inspire and connect with readers on a profound level. Alongside his husband, Thomas, a talented artist and psychology professional, Robert envisions a future where they can open a small clinic together, offering psychological support and creative expression to those in need.

In his free time, Robert enjoys exploring the mountains and beaches, collecting antiques, and sharing life's beautiful moments with his husband and their tuxedo cat, Domino.

Bibliography

While Timeless Connections is a work of fiction, Robert's understanding of human behavior and emotional depth is informed by his studies in clinical psychology and his lived experiences. His academic pursuits and personal journey have shaped his ability to write characters that are both complex and relatable.

Sources for inspiration and themes include:

- Life experiences in the LGBTQ+ community.
- The pursuit of authenticity and self-discovery.
- The power of love in overcoming life's challenges.
- Psychological and emotional growth through hardship.